<u>AMBROSIAL</u>

Soumik R. Chakraborty

Dedicated to my Mother and Father

What makes a man, a man? A friend of mine once asked. Is it his origins? The way he comes to life? I don't think so. It's the choices he makes. Not how he starts things, but how he decides to end them - John Myers, Hellboy (2004)

PART 1: OF LAB COATS, WHITE MICE AND SAFETY GOGGLES

A few of us were standing on the sixth-floor balcony of a six storied building. The premises had been designated as the smoking area for the entire building. Thankfully the open air allowed the thick clouds of cigarette smoke to dissipate, without obscuring the vision of the smokers. All of us were either taking a break from the monotony of work, trying to psych ourselves up before a conference call, or merely trying to inhale a cigarette in one long drag, like an animated dragon fueling up on ammunition, before stepping back inside and taking on a particularly daunting assignment. When you work in high stress environments and you are a smoker, having either picked up the habit after you started working or sometime earlier in life, you tend to set up a reward system for yourself. After every hour, your gift to yourself, for the hard work that you have done, is going out to the balcony and grabbing a smoke. Somehow even your smoke breaks become organized and planned; you buy a pack of twenty cigarettes while coming to office in the morning, and set out your smoke breaks such that the empty crumbled packet finds its way to the dustbin under your workstation at the end of the day. On most days you work for up to sixteen to eighteen hours anyway, and sometimes you may even cheat on your smoke breaks by sneaking in two cigarettes in place of one. Sometimes those cigarettes are mint flavored if you prefer the cooling sensation and are brave enough to take a deeper drag without paying heed to sexist rumors, perpetuated by misogynists, that menthol cigarettes cause your testicles to shrink. The anti-smoking lobby in the building had run a tireless and unceasing campaign to have the area closed off to smokers, so that they could breathe cleaner air, but us worshippers of tobacco had emerged bruised, battered and crippled by temporary withdrawal, but victorious in the end. We had succeeded in keeping the balcony open for smoking and the flames of our coffin nails burning. The cigarette fumes, as they slowly killed us, smelt like freedom. Cue "More Than A Feeling" by Boston.

I was in the midst of my first smoke of the day, trying to psych myself up before stepping back into the office and sitting down to a particularly excruciating session of document diligence. Back then I happened to work for a law firm that was, and still is, according to numerous listicles on the internet, one of the best in the country. I worked in the capital markets team, a practice area that is extremely time consuming and diligence intensive, with a milestone-based billing system. This essentially means that even if you are killing yourself with work and spending sleepless nights in the office, the total number of billable hours you put in does not matter. The firm gets paid only if specific pre-determined milestones are completed in the transaction, and not in accordance with the amount of time you spend staring into a computer.

While mentally chalking out my game plan on how to approach the work at hand, I ran into a friend of mine, Xeala. She worked in the same firm but with a different team and in the private equity practice area. I had seen her during my first week of orientation, talking the ears off of an associate who had come on a temporary deputation from Japan, and had thought to myself that here was one girl with whom I would probably never become friends. I had an inherent aversion to loquacious people. However, by a very serendipitous turn of events, Xeala and I discovered that we had common friends. The revelation occurred when we ran into each other at a common friend's birthday party, a couple of months into the start of our jobs. By temperament and in our tastes, we could not have been more different, yet somehow, we clicked together. Very soon, both of us became very close friends.

"How many has it been today?" Xeala asked when she spotted me standing in a corner blowing smoke out of my nose with a faraway look in my eyes.

"Oh hey!" I said, having been brought back to earth, "this is my first one." I held up the cigarette to my face and surveyed it with mock curiosity, as if I was seeing it for the first time and had no idea how it came to be placed between my index and middle fingers.

"Yeah right," she said and rolled her eyes at me, "what is happening?"

"Nothing much," I said, "dying with work". This was a template response that nearly all of us, who worked in the firm, ended up giving as an instinctive answer, whenever anyone asked us about our state of affairs. A drinking game based on the number of times a colleague gives you such an identical answer in a day would surely cause all the participants in the game to die from alcohol poisoning.

"Aww..." Xeala sympathized, "it will get better," she said patting my hand.

I was a sucker for the "awwws" and like a cat mollified by a human stroking its head, I could feel my trepidation at taking up my upcoming daunting assignment ebbing away. "Let's hope so," I said, "what brings you here?"

"Taking a long-deserved break from my transaction. It seems that I can get out from work early today. The transaction has tanked."

Tanked was the colloquial word we used in the firm to indicate that a transaction has come to a full stop, that it will not be moving forward and has no chance of being revived at any time in the future. Such news was the equivalent of finding out that your terminal illness has been miraculously cured.

"Woah, what happened?" I was curious.

"The foreign investors backed out. The start-up they were planning to fund has become a toxic asset. Apparently, the engineers did not have the privacy policy uploaded on the company's website and such an omission will open it up to lawsuits in the future for violation of data privacy and selling private user information to other corporations." Xeala said.

"But the start-up would have still been mining user data anyway, would it have not?" I asked.

"Of course, it would have, but the privacy policy would have acted like caveat emptor, a buyer beware provision. Users would be voluntarily providing personal information but the policy would state something to the effect that the app has absolute control over how it uses such data and the users cannot take any legal action against them. Sort of a catch-all that would protect the start-up from angry users, like a 'Hey, we told you that we were going to misappropriate your private data but you voluntarily gave it to us anyway.'"

I sniggered as I remembered a joke I had read somewhere, about how internet companies can trick you into signing over the title deed to your home when you click "I agree" on the terms of services, since no one actually takes time to go through the shrink wrap in detail. Xeala raised an eyebrow and looked at me. I shook my head.

"Nothing." I said, "Just remembered something funny. Well, what can you do? Someone's loss, someone's gain. The start-up loses out on, what I am guessing, a sizeable investment and you get to leave office early for once." I said.

Xeala tapped her nose to indicate agreement. "They were really hoping to become a unicorn with that cash infusion."

"A billion-dollar valuation even before their initial public offering?" I asked, my eyes bulging in surprise.

"Yep. I missed out on being a part of history." said Xeala, shrugging with slight nonchalance.

"What is the company called?" I asked.

"Ungle" she replied.

"Uncle?" I asked, confused.

"No, Ungle" Xeala said, touching the tip of her tongue to the roof of her mouth to hit the hard 'g'.

"What?!" I could not help laughing, "What kind of a name is that?"

"These nouveau entrepreneurs have some pretty crazy rituals when coming up with names of their companies. It seems that there is some sort of guidebook for start-up founders that advises them to name their company after something primal, like the first words that come out of your mouth when you reach climax, hence Unnggle" she said, imitating a man reaching completion.

"Ah!" I said.

"And some others go on vision quests. Take a lot of hallucinogens and go sit some-where quiet while they wait for their inner eye to open up and a revolutionary name to pop into their head."

"That is in the guidebook too?" I asked, "That is how members of the Great Race of Yith tend to switch bodies with you when you are in tripping on high quality peyote and your mind is too addled to resist." I said with a straight face.

"What is the Great Race of Yith?" asked Xeala

"Aliens from the planet Pluto, who switch minds with creatures across time and space in order to study them." I clarified, "But it does make you wonder at times, whether having ordinary ambitions with an ordinary life plan would have been better. Barley scrape through college and school with the minimum qualifications, pass some exam for employment with the government that guarantees job security, get married at twenty-eight, raise a couple of kids and pass on the same values to them."

"Maybe." she shrugged.

"Anyway, what does Ungle," I made sure that I replicated Xeala's pronunciation, "do?"

"It is a pharmaceutical company, specializing in anti-aging technology. They also act as an aggregator of transfusion associates."

"What's that?" I asked

"Blood donors for the rich. It is an experimental procedure by which transfusion of small quantities of blood from a healthy younger donor to an older recipient helps to slow down the ageing process by supplying the body with newer and more efficient cell organelles."

"Is it medically approved?" I asked, slightly horrified.

"They have been chasing the authorities for approval. The funding would have granted them legitimacy and made their case stronger." Xeala said.

"You work with interesting companies." I said, slightly jealous, once the initial horror had worn off.

"Blood Bag Inc. certainly has been the wildest one yet. Anyway, do you want to grab a drink?" she asked.

"I would love to get a drink," I said, stubbing out my cigarette, "it has been two weeks since I have gone anywhere in a social capacity. I spent the last couple of Fridays being in office till 2 am, stuck on a high-pressure transaction for issuance of global depository receipts on the New York Stock Exchange. The deal closed day before, and it is been relatively light work in office ever since. Let me see if I can get out early today." I said.

"Did you guys make it to the front page of the Financial Times?" she teased. This was the biggest incentive that we were given, as corporate lawyers, that the deals we worked on were cutting edge front page worthy transactions and would be responsible for changing the face of the world economy. It was the first time that I had heard the phrase cutting edge being used in the context of something that did not involve lab coats, white mice and safety goggles. The incentive was an exaggeration, since we were mentioned barely as an afterthought in those articles. If the corporations were the police, us lawyers were the vigilante caped crusaders. Only the police got the glory, the recognition and the photographs in the papers while we continued to be looked down upon as the scourge of society.

"We did not," I pouted, "it was quite a small transaction, time consuming but small nevertheless. Not paper worthy, front page or anywhere." I said, lamenting not being inducted into the hallowed halls of narcissism.

"Oh... that is too bad," she consoled me, "you will get the glory for the next one maybe. Anyway, let me know if you can make it. I am planning to leave by 7:30 p.m."

"I will." said I, giving her a side hug and going back inside.

After killing ourselves for the past two weeks on the global depository receipts transaction, even my reporting senior wanted to get out early that day. Her boyfriend was in town and was waiting for her back in her home. She had a nice apartment on the sixteenth floor of a sea shore adjacent building. I had been there only once for a party. The view from her balcony was amazing and such sights on moonlit nights accompanied with smooth jazz music, could turn the most prosaic person into an acclaimed poet. My senior was more than happy to call the day to an early close and relieved me so that I could keep my appointment with Xeala.

Both Xeala and I enjoyed greasy food with our beers, especially if it was nachos and cheesy fries. We were looking to try out a new place that day and found one called Señor Chiquita a few hundred meters from the office.

The interior of the restaurant had been decorated by someone who had personally never experienced Latin American culture and had only seen it through the movies of Robert Rodriguez. Posters of Antonio Banderas dressed as a mariachi with long hair, carrying the infamous guitar case full of guns, while walking on a highway, adorned two walls, one each from Desperado and its sequel Once Upon A Time In Mexico. A few Clint Eastwood posters had been thrown into the mix, and some sombreros were hung at random places. There was one poster of Danny Trejo with his coat open, wearing a Navajo vest underneath, with a mean expression on his face.

You could almost hear him saying "You just messed with the wrong Mexican." The whole restaurant was lit with tungsten bulbs, which made the place quite warm. We felt like we were *actually* in extremely hot tropical climate. The best way to describe the decor of the place was Latino Spaghetti Western. The only thing missing was a live mariachi band to interrupt us during conversations, but such lacuna was compensated with the soothing music of acoustic guitars with seductive voices crooning in Spanish, that played over the sound system in the restaurant. The music was faint and mostly ambient without overwhelming the auditory senses. We were thankful for it because most other establishments providing similar services as Señor Chiquita have the volume turned up to eleven and you can end up losing your voice the next day, ironically from all the shouting to make yourself heard, rather than because of the chilled beer.

We found a table, sat down, and in defiance to our surroundings, ordered a couple of German beers, as well as a plate nacho with all the fixings. The dish appeared to be a popular offering of the restaurant, and consisted of nachos drenched in cheese sauce, and topped off with every add-ons that Señor Chiquita had to offer.

Xeala was a very considerate friend. She had recently started going out with a guy named Axxen who was introduced to her by a common friend. The guy was showering her with chocolates much like Cleopatra showered those, who earned her favour, in gold. Xeala did not know this yet, as they were barely a few months into the relationship, and she used to tell me that it was just a fling for her, but she and her boyfriend would end up dating for nearly five years and would soon contemplate marriage.

Now Xeala had made it her life's mission to set me up with someone as well. Things were not helped by my telling Xeala that during an office party, a few weeks earlier, my senior, in a state of semi-inebriation, had taken me aside and told me that I needed to find someone to date if I was to survive in the firm, someone who could act as my physical and emotional support, someone who would be by my side through the good times and the bad times. This was something Xeala completely agreed upon with my boss, and since I was not seeing anyone at the moment, Xeala had taken it upon herself to find someone for me.

"So", Xeala began, after permitting the obligatory five minutes to be spent in talking about inconsequential things after we seated ourselves, before she could bring up the topic again, "Did you see someone you like in office?". It was slightly disconcerting for me to note that she had not asked whether I had "met someone", but whether I had "seen someone", like she was my co-conspirator in a stalking ploy. After having put Xeala off for close to two months, I finally had an answer in the affirmative for her.

"As a matter of fact, I did," I said, "saw her a couple of days ago on the fifth floor, working in the finance team. Your floor actually. I asked around and found out her name is Sandxira. Apparently, she had joined with us, but I do not recollect having seen her in orientation." I said.

For the uninitiated, orientation was a five-day long affair that happened on the very first week after new recruits joined the firm. The partners of the firm were brought in to speak with us, apprise us of the teams that they headed, the kind of work the firm did and the quality of work and commitment that was expected of us. This was followed by various other sessions, such as grooming sessions that taught us obscure rituals like power dressing, and other ice breaker sessions that were intended for us to get to know our colleagues and platonically fraternise with them. By the end of it, it felt like we were one-incantation-from-a-human-flesh-bound-book-to-invoke-an-Elder-God away from being inducted into a cult.

"Really? Was she not at orientation? What does she look like?" Xeala asked.

"Well, I glanced at her fleetingly," I said, "but I remember that she has long curly hair that comes down to her elbows and a caramel like complexion, shifting towards fair, not that I see those kind of things," I clarified hastily to Xeala, and for the benefit of any person who might be offended by reading such description, "she wears square glasses, has thin artistic fingers and umm..." I hesitated, "is endowed well."

Xeala raised her eyebrows at me.

"She was dressed that day, when I saw her, in white shirt and black trousers. She has a toothy welcoming smile." I finished off

"That is more than a fleeting glance, stalker." Xeala teased.

"You are right, I was being modest. To be honest, she is quite," I paused for dramatic effect, and because I was looking for the applicable word, "alluring." I finished.

"You are such a trickster. All these times you made false promises to me that I am your number one girl." Xeala said, her lips pouting.

"You are my number one girl Xeala. If your chocolate guy bails on you or hurts you, I will be there for you in a heartbeat." I said, a thin smile on my lips.

Xeala punched me playfully.

"So, have you decided how you are going to approach this woman, Sandxira did you say her name was?" she asked.

"I am not sure if I will. Never been lucky with women." I said, "I pined after this one girl who was in my class in college for five years without building up the courage to say anything to her. I am not sure if I have it in me to pine for a few more years after this Sandxira woman."

"Oh yeah? What happened to that woman you were pining for?

In the meantime, our food and drinks had arrived. It took every ounce of self-control that I could muster to draw myself away from the enticing aroma of the nachos, and answer Xeala.

"I don't know, man." I said, "She and I became very good friends for a brief period, kind of like you and I are right now. But then she started dating this guy she had met through some common friends, and for some strange reason I told her that her boyfriend appeared to be untrustworthy."

"Did you actually have reason to believe that he was untrustworthy?" Xeala asked.

"Not really. It was just an assumption that I made about him. Call it an intuition if you will. One that did fail me in hindsight, probably."

This time the punch from Xeala really hurt.

"You idiot. You never say such things to a woman. Even if chances are that the guy may not be a good person. Women are incredibly defensive of the people they date and you have to let them come to the realization themselves whether someone is a douchebag or not instead of poking your nose in their business."

"That's fair. I realize that now. Having said that, it will not prevent me from making fun of chocolate guy. I am totally going to do that any chance that I get."

"Come on. I concede that he is a little odd, but he seems like a sweet guy otherwise. I cannot go out for drinks with him though as he is a teetotaler and has no vices, unlike the other company I keep." she said, looking at me in a mischievous manner, "Anyway, what are you going to do about Sandxira?"

"I am planning to take a glacial approach." I said.

"What's that?" Xeala asked.

"I intend to wait for the glaciers to melt, for the seas to finally rise and drown everything, cause a mass extinction event, and only then I will finally have the confidence to approach her, so that is when I intend to ask her out."

"You can piss off." said Xeala and pulled out her phone. She opened her social media account, browsed briefly and found Sandxira's profile. Xeala excitedly thrust her phone in my face.

"What am I looking at?" I asked, through a mouthful of nachos.

"She appears to have studied at a law school that is in your home city, Idiot! There is your in. Tell her that you are from the same city and start talking. I am pretty sure that will be a good ice breaker."

"You are optimistic." I said, and took a swig of beer. Xeala's beer lay forgotten, drunk half way. Condensed water was dripping down the side of the bottle and had created a pool at the bottom. A stream of water from the pool had started to flow out and had almost reached the bowl of peanuts that the waiter had brought as a complimentary side dish with the beers.

"I am telling you that it is going to work." Xeala admonished me for my lack of faith.

"I might give it a try. Will have to find an excuse to see her though." I said.

"I'll tell you how to go about it. On the coming Monday, why don't you come down to the fifth floor, walk to her desk and start a conversation with her, like a normal person. In the course of it, let her know that you are meeting me for lunch in the cafeteria. Then you can ask her to join us." said Xeala, "You will find it easier to talk to her in a group and it will also give me an opportunity to check her out and see if she's a good fit for you."

"Awwww... that is so sweet of you, Xeala, looking out for me." I said.

"You did call me your number one girl, and I take my duty very seriously. That is, till the time Sandxira takes the spot, at which point you and I are through."

"Fair enough! Sounds like a plan," I said, "but it is contingent on a massive 'if', which is you being available for lunch and being able to get away from your desk without your senior dumping work on you."

"I am sure I will manage somehow," Xeala assured me, "Just don't choke up when speaking to her."

"I will try my best." said I giving a non-comital shrug.

The lazy tunes of 'La Pistola y el Corazon' floated in the background.

PART 2: BYE BYE BYE

During lunch hour the following Monday, I found myself gliding down the stairs to the fifth floor from my hallowed sixth, planning to put Xeala's plan into action and ask Sandxira to join us for lunch.

As I approached Sandxira's desk, it felt surreal. Even though I had barely known her and never spoken to her ever, I had inadvertently built Sandxira up in my head as someone I would be too intimidated to speak with. My mouth was becoming dry and my heart was thumping really fast in my chest. A part of my brain was trying to come up with a perfect analogy for my situation and the best one my morbid mind could come up with was that if I was a dead body in a gothic horror story, this would be the time when my killer would pull up the floorboards to reveal my desiccated corpse to the police, which he had hidden underneath, my loudly thumping telltale heart having given him away.

I approached Sandxira's desk, and instead of the words, "Hi" coming out, I managed to make a garbled sound, courtesy of the phlegm in my throat. Smoking twenty cigarettes a day makes your throat work overtime to repair the damage caused by nicotine and causes you to be perpetually stuck with the affliction of having to clear your throat before speaking.

She looked up at the sound, and saw me. That's when I finally managed to say "Hi".

"Oh hi!" she said brightly.

From here on, I introduced myself and told Sandxira that I worked a floor above her in the capital markets practice. She was quite friendly and told me that she had joined the finance practice about the same time as Xeala and I. Over the course of our conversation, I asked her about not having seen her at orientation, and she told me that she was a lateral hire who had not joined with the other new recruits. It seemed that she had prior work experience with another firm. However, when I asked her to join me for lunch, she smiled and politely declined my request. She said that she had just been staffed on a new transaction and had to get started with some research.

That was one more unpleasant thing about working in such a place as I did. You have to forego any semblance of routine or a regular life since you are expected cancel all your plans to undertake work at the drop of a hat. Lunch plans were regularly jeopardized and feelings were frequently hurt. The origin stories of many a sympathetic super-villain was birthed in the firm.

I resigned myself to heading out to the cafeteria alone and settled down heavily in a chair next to Xeala.

"Where's Sandxira?" she asked. I apprised her of the absentee's predicament.

"Cheer up," she said. "Basuretta has made your favourite okra for lunch today." I looked up to see our perpetually cheerful cafeteria-in-charge, Basuretta, waving at me. The man was a ray of pure sunshine. Five minutes spent chatting with him could pull one out of the deepest throes of mental anguish, so infectious was his enthusiasm for life. He was the human equivalent of a P.G. Wodehouse novel, which, incidentally happen to be the best non-medicated anti-depressants of all time. He was also a big gossiper and had dirt on nearly everyone in the office.

Shortly after he had seen me come in, Basuretta walked over and pulled a chair up to our table. After a few adjustments, he was able to fit his thin wiry frame into the chair.

"How are you Sir? We rarely see you on the fifth floor these days." said the man. He addressed everyone by Sir. It never felt sycophantic and seemed genuinely respectful. He had told us on countless occasions how he had immense respect for lawyers, and that was one of the main reasons he had sought out a job in our office, wanting to see lawyers up close in action.

"What can I say Basuretta Sir," I said, not one to exercise restraint when it came to being courteous, "work has been hectic these past few days. We never get a chance to have lunch at a decent hour. You usually leave by the time I come in."

"Oh! I am sorry to hear that Sir." Said Basuretta, "I hope it is better now. I miss seeing you."

"Thanks, Basuretta Sir. You are missed too. It is better, slightly. Let us see how long it lasts. You can never predict things with this place."

"Wait, I will get you some okra. Xeala madam has been telling me how much you love it." Saying so, Basuretta laboriously extricated himself from the chair. He walked to the kitchen and came back a short while later, carrying a white plastic bowl filled to the brim with fried okra. He laid the bowl in front of me and promptly seated himself again.

"Basuretta, do you know this girl on the fifth floor called Sandxira?" Xeala chipped in.

"Ahh... Sandxira madam? I have seen her around but she rarely comes to lunch. Slightly short lady with curly hair and square glasses, am I right?" asked Basuretta, Xeala looked at me and smiled.

"Yes, that's her." confirmed Xeala.

"I do not know madam. She usually keeps to herself. Seems to always be busy in work like you," Basuretta indicated me, "she does not appear to have many friends either. Why do you ask?"

"Your Sir here," said Xeala, pointing at me, "has a little crush on her."

"No, I have not." I protested instinctively, feeling my ears going red. No matter how old you get, you never grow out of your school boy like embarrassment at having your secret crush revealed.

"Ahahaha!" said Basuretta, "she is pretty. Do you want me to speak with her? Get you some inside intel?"

Xeala burst out laughing at Basuretta's enthusiasm and my gradually increasing embarrassment.

"Come on Basuretta Sir! Even you are pulling my leg now!" I said.

"Not at all Sir. Just command me and I shall do the job."

"Its okay, Basuretta Sir. Thank you for your kind offer, but I am fine for now. I will reach out to you if I need any intel."

"Suit yourself Sir, but time is running out for you." said Basuretta, as he surreptitiously eyed my slightly greying hairline. I gave an awkward guffaw. At that moment Basuretta saw someone else come into the cafeteria; someone else who needed his daily dose of Basuretta sunshine. He took our leave to attend to that person. The moment Basuretta left, I turned to Xeala, faux fire blazing in my eyes.

"What was that?" I asked Xeala incredulously.

"Come on! I was just having a little fun with you." said Xeala.

"Why would you say all that to Basuretta? He is the biggest gossiper in the office! He will go around saying all that stuff about me crushing on Sandxira and any realistic hope that I may have about asking her out will be dead on arrival. She'll think that I am some sort of a creep."

"You do have a crush on her, don't you?"

"That's beside the point, Xeala!"

"Come on."

I paused for a few moments and let my agitation subside. "Well," I said, "to be honest with you, she is like the woman in the red dress that the machines have custom designed for me, to distract me from realizing my true potential, figuring out about the grim reality of the Matrix, and becoming humanity's messiah."

"Again, with the pop culture references," Xeala shook her head in disdain, "anyway Basuretta won't say anything. I will speak with him." Xeala assured me. She reached over and scooped up some fried okra with a spoon.

"With you around to help me, waiting for melting glaciers and rising seas won't be long enough." I said. Xeala made a face at me.

~

After that day, I ran into Sandxira on a few other occasions. Sometimes she came up to our balcony on the sixth floor for a break and a stroll. She did not smoke, but did not mind the smell of tobacco either. A few times I saw her leaving the cafeteria as I went in to have lunch with Xeala whenever the latter could make time. On those occasions, Sandxira and I idly chatted. She told me about herself. Turned out that she did know a lot about my home city, and in the five years of law school had travelled around the place extensively. The law school benefited from being situated right in the middle of the city and was easily accessible by public transports, as opposed to other law schools in the country, which were situated far away from the city, at distances encompassing entire star systems. Sandxira was easy to talk to, and I found, to my slight surprise, that very few awkward silences filled in the gaps between our conversations. Sandxira said that even though she was not a native of my home city, she found the place quite warm, charming and hospitable, compliments that made me quite happy. She confessed that it was on her bucket list to travel an entire day in the trams that plied through the city, an experience she had not had enough of while in law school. She wanted to just get on a tram and travel from one end of the city to the other. I told her that if she and I were ever in the city at the same time, I would love to accompany her on such tram rides, so long as she did not mind me gushing eloquent about the sites of the city, like a well-meaning, but slightly obnoxious tour guide. Sandxira laughed when she heard this, a very throaty and lilting laugh at the same time. She did not appear to be patronizing me, but genuinely found what I had said to be humorous.

A few weeks later it was my birthday, and Xeala was planning a special outing. It was the first birthday that I was going to spend at my new job. It was not the first time that I would be spending a birthday away from home, having spent five years of law school in one of the southern cities of the country, with my birthday falling on a date that was always very close to the even semester examinations. However, Xeala wanted to make it special. She came from a family where birthdays had always been a big deal and were required to be celebrated properly. As far as I was concerned, she had already set the bar quite high for herself by surprising me with a home cooked meal the previous night, something that was truly luxurious, in our erstwhile culture of working late hours and mostly ordering out. Xeala wanted the celebrations to continue and wanted to take me out for drinks later in the evening, along with some common friends that she would be inviting over.

In a rookie move, I suggested that she could invite Sandxira over as well. Xeala's face hardened momentarily, but she acquiesced to what the birthday boy had requested and called Sandxira. I realized too late that Xeala wanted the party to be an intimate affair and was hesitant to invite a relative stranger. But her concerns were taken care of, as it turned out that Sandxira would not be able to make it that day either, since she had some prior commitments.

I ran into Sandxira the next morning and was surprised by a greeting of "Belated happy returns of the day, birthday boy" from her, followed by a hug. I fumbled when saying thanks and felt the colours rising in my cheek. She looked radiant as she smiled at me. Needless to say, that was the highlight of my mediocre day.

Soon, close to a year had passed. I still knew as much about my job as bastard men, born of illegitimate union in medieval fantasy novels, knew about anything. I was merely going through the motions and following a monotonous routine. I was like a protagonist from a Nine Inch Nails song, bemoaning about every day being exactly the same. The few bright things about my life were my friendship with Xeala and my talks with Sandxira. She and I were not close friends yet, more like work-proximity associates, but we did seem to enjoy each other's company.

However, the status quo was not meant to last. Xeala realized that working in a law firm was not what she wanted to do for the rest of her life, and decided to leave the job to pursue her other goal in life, of trying and becoming a bureaucrat, which would require her to pass the extremely grueling civil services examination.

Saying goodbye to her was one of the most difficult goodbyes I ever had to say in my life. Xeala was one of the few things that was keeping me grounded, keeping my sanity in place, and stopping me from going on a self-destructive path. Both of us could understand each other's predicaments and found comfort in each other. We did not always need beer on the table, to be able to tell one another how terrible a day each of us had had. We just needed a few minutes with each other to speak and vent every day.

On the weekend before she left the city, Xeala's roommate and I conspired and roped in a few close friends to throw her a going away party at her home. It was a treat to watch her eyes bulge in surprise as she saw us huddled outside her front door, holding packets of foods and beer bottles in our hands. After everyone had settled in and a round of beer had been finished by the attendees, Xeala dragged me away from the party and took me downstairs. We stepped outside her apartment complex where we could finally have some privacy. It was not completely unexpected but I was still taken aback, when she hugged me tightly, her body pressed against mine. She held on to me and refused to let go. We held on to each other under the shade of a tree, hidden away from the glare of the streetlights. Thirty Mississippis later, we finally broke apart.

"Are you okay?" I asked.

"Yes." said Xeala and then she gave a slight sniff.

I stroked her head as she looked at me and smiled. She closed her eyes and enjoyed my caressing.

"What's up? Is something troubling you?" I asked.

"I am slightly worried." she said and let out a sigh.

I waited for her to go on.

"I don't know man, I am beginning to wonder if quitting my job to pursue the civil service examinations, was the correct choice." she continued.

"What's with all the self-doubt?" I asked.

"I had a routine here." Xeala said, "wake up in the morning, go to office, complain about work, come back nearly dead from exhaustion, go to back to sleep and wake up again the next morning. At the end of the month, I was assured of a sizeable pay check."

"You mean retainer fees."

Xeala looked at me with scorn.

"I digress," I said, slightly abashed, "but go on."

"And now I am looking at an uncertain future, relying on my savings to prepare for an examination whose outcome is beyond my control. I am beginning to wonder if it will all be worth it."

"I thought this is what you wanted." I said.

"I did, but then I keep having second thoughts about it."

I sighed, took the packet of cigarettes out of my pocket and lit one. I let out a gust of smoke and looked at Xeala. "Come, let us sit over there." I said, pointing to a tree that was encircled by a cemented sitting area. We walked over and sat down. I continued to puff on my cigarette. I placed my hand around Xeala's shoulder and held her to me tightly.

"Xeala, I don't know what is going to happen. I am not in a position to tell you how everything will turn out. Least of all, I should not even be telling you what to do with your life. I am not being melodramatic here, but the day you told me you were leaving, it broke my heart. I am the last person who wants to see you go away."

Xeala snuggled closer to me and buried her face in my chest.

"Having said that, I admire your courage for going after what you want. I am excited that you are trying something new. I wish I had your guts. I wish I could go after what I want and not become an old man filled with regrets. Whatever happens, and I am sure it will happen for the best, you will come out the other side a stronger person. Unless you break free of your comfort zone, you will not know exactly how much you are capable of, will you?"

A slight muffled groan escaped from Xeala.

"And this will be great for your relationship with Axxen. I mean, he seems happy for you, right? He is there to support you and he is willing to wait with you. Plus, he will always be there to comfort you with chocolates."

"He is a great guy.' said Xeala, finally lifting her head. There were a couple of tiny wet patches on my shirt.

"The best. And he does not smoke or drink, so high life expectancy and great genes are a given."

Xeala slapped my free arm, and then laid her head on my shoulder. We sat there in silence for a while. Traffic on the road slowly began to thin as the night got deeper. A sweeper had come out to get a head start on his job. A few taxis were whizzing past us, some of them empty, some of them filled with people heading out to late night parties. Snatches of conversation could be heard in bursts.

I began humming 'The Last Waltz', a tune that I had heard in a Korean movie once. I did not know the name of the haunting tune back then and had to look it up online, but it left a lasting impact on me. I had hummed it so many times around Xeala that she knew the tune well and waited for me to finish before saying anything.

"Thanks," she said, "this meant a lot to me."

"Of course, anything for you." I said and kissed her on the head.

We got up from the bench and began to walk back to her home. The party began to empty out shortly after we returned. I waited till the end and helped Xeala and her roommate clean up the place. Xeala and I hugged once more before I left. As I got into the elevator of her apartment building and started descending, she blew me a kiss and I smiled.

~

A few weeks later, Sandxira told me that she was leaving as well. Serendipitously, she had found a job that would be taking her back to my home city. She said that she was bored after working for a year in the law firm and wanted to explore other opportunities.

It was now or never, a Hail Mary moment, a time to throw caution to the wind and pop the question. I had run scenarios of this in my mind before and hoped that she would not be completely averse to considering the possibility.

I braced myself and asked her.

"Hey, I know you are here for only another couple of weeks, but would you ever consider going out with me?"

Sandxira stood like a deer caught in headlights for a few moments. Then I saw the left corner of her mouth twitching. The twitching slowly transformed into a smile, and then she said, "I am very flattered, but unfortunately I cannot."

"Oh...", I said, "I see, that's cool. Umm... Good Luck with your future pursuits then. Hope you find what you are looking for."

Saying this, I turned around and began walking away, slightly despondent.

"Wait." she said.

I turned around, a quizzical look on my face.

"Is that it? You don't have any follow up questions about why I cannot go out with you?" Sandxira asked.

"I presume you are seeing someone already or maybe you have some other compulsions?" I ventured a guess.

"Ahh... that is not it." Sandxira said.

"Umm... then what is the reason?"

Sandxira said, "You would be coming down home, on leave, right? Why don't you look me up when you are there, and we can speak about it?"

"Umm... okay, that's cool. Fair enough." I said, and walked away.

My head was a maelstrom of emotions. On the one hand I was slightly annoyed to be turned down so bluntly, and on the other hand, I felt elated that Sandxira wanted to continue to keep in touch with me even after leaving her job. It meant that she thought of me as more than a work-proximity associate. Corny though it sounds, her suggestion to look her up when I was back home, made me feel elated. After that day, I barely saw Sandxira.

PART 3: JEEVES TO THE RESCUE

After both Xeala and Sandxira left, it felt odd being in the office. I had other friends as well, but I did not have an active social life. Because of the flustered manner in which I left things with Sandxira before saying goodbye, I had not managed to procure her contact number. Xeala gave it to me a few days later as a delayed parting gift.

It had been a few months since Sandxira left, but I had not had the chance to message her. It was partly because I was too busy with work and spent nearly all my breaks decompressing, and partly because I felt apprehensive, as I was not sure if she had truly meant to keep in touch or was just being polite.

Finally building up courage, I messaged her one day, saying "Hi". I immediately put my phone away and switched off the mobile data, treating my phone like Schrödinger's cat. Till the time the data was switched off, I would not know whether a reply from Sandxira had or had not come into my phone.

I waited for five minutes, and then picked up my phone. I switched on the mobile data, and quickly locked my screen. Immediately my screen lit up with a message from Sandxira that said "Hey".

It turned out that she was prompt with her replies to my messages, and we ended up texting for quite a while that day. She brought me up to speed about her new office, its excellent location, about the work she was doing and how her co-workers were. Sandxira also told me, in particular, about an over eager colleague. This colleague had confided in Sandxira about having trouble at home trying to convince the former's parents about getting married to a man of a different religious faith. Somehow Sandxira had gotten sucked into the drama.

"Why don't you suggest to her to take the Jeeves approach?" I messaged.

"What is that?" she wrote back.

"It's a guerrilla advertising method known as direct suggestion."

"How does that work?"

"It consists of driving an idea home by constant repetition, like an advertisement telling you that a soap manufactured by a particular company, who happens to be paying for the advertisement, is the best. That such soap will be the most suitable for moisturizing your skin, removing your pimples and making your skin glow."

"Hahaha. Go on :)" Sandxira messaged back.

"The advertisement keeps on repeating the same properties of the soap on a loop till you come under its influence, become convinced by the qualities of the soap and charge around the corner to the grocer's shop, where you immediately buy a cake of it."

"And how will that help this woman?"

"Your friend could use this concept to her advantage. In the story that I am referring to, the beleaguered protagonist reads stories to his elderly rich uncle about star crossed lovers from different strata of society, who are cruelly torn apart by the constraints of social order but are eventually reunited. Our protagonist needs his uncle's blessings because he is in love with a waitress and wants his uncle to increase his allowance so that he can get married to his paramour."

"Has our protagonist not heard of a job?" Sandxira wrote back.

"These are wealthy aristocrats and members of the idle rich, living off the wealth accumulated through generations." I messaged.

"I see. By the way, is Jeeves the name of the protagonist?"

"Uh... no, that would be Bingo Little. Jeeves is the valet of a friend of his, who comes up with the whole idea. He is an extremely intelligent, resourceful, well-read, efficient and articulate valet, kind of like Sherlock Holmes and Alfred Pennyworth had a child together. A very unique character."

"Sounds intriguing."

"He is. Anyway, the stories melt the uncle's heart, who till then, had staunchly been against marriage between people of different classes. The old man is so warmed by the tales that he enters into matrimonial union himself, with his housekeeper. Unfortunately for the protagonist, the whole scheme backfires as the uncle now needs the additional money that his nephew was hoping to squeeze out of him, to support him and his newlywed wife. Our hero is left in the same position that he was before, and with the same allowance, not a penny more, not a penny less."

"Hahaha!"

"Your friend could do something similar, you know, by reading to her parents or telling them stories about marriages between people of different faiths, and how such marriages have been lovely, blessed and happy unions. It will be bound to soften their hearts and make them come to terms with their own daughter's impending inter faith nuptials. And it goes without saying, I hope it ends on a happier note for her."

"Interesting. This is a novel approach worth trying out." Sandxira messaged, "Do you have any such books or stories that I can suggest to my friend for reference?"

"Mostly stories about honor killings." I wrote back, "But I am hopeful that she will be able to undertake the research herself, now that I have provided the basis on which to proceed." I wrote back.

"Hahahaha. Fair enough. I will pass on your idea. Maybe she will invite you to her wedding for your path breaking suggestion, if it actually works, and you and I can go together." Wrote Sandxira.

"Hahaha (sweat emoji). I look forward to it. Hopefully it will not end in a red wedding. Won't be able to afford the higher premium of insurance if I am killed."

"Or worse, expelled ;)"

That day I ended up being stuck in office till 3 am, because my deliverables got delayed by a couple of hours, on account of my chat fest with Sandxira. Very few things in life are worth such hardships, and this was one of them.

~

A few days later, I told Xeala about what had transpired with Sandxira. I was sitting on the bed at my rented flat, looking out of a window at the slowly reddening sky, as Saturday came to a close. Xeala registered the excitement in my voice and was quick to deflate my enthusiasm.

"Calm down, she just said all that because she was flirting with you. It could be entirely harmless. It especially does not mean that she is planning ahead for her friend's imaginary wedding, and wants to bring you along, especially a wedding whose future depends on the execution and success of such an outlandish scheme." Xeala said.

"Hmm... I know. It is not like I was on cloud nine or anything, but this is what I find confusing. Why did she say that she could not go out with me, but suggested the whole wedding thing? It surely means that she is open to making plans that involve me."

"Do not overthink this." said Xeala, "Like I said, she was caught up in the moment. The chances of her friend inviting you to her wedding at all, in the first place, is astronomical."

"Hmm..." I pondered aloud.

"For all you know, Sandxira could be a cog in this huge uncaring machine called life, who just happened to cross paths with you, and you became enticed with her. Maybe there is no deeper meaning to all of this."

"Why are you being so cynical?"

"I am busting chops today. That's my thing." Xeala replied.

"Yeah, fair enough. I see what you mean," I said, "anyway, how is it going with the chocolate guy?"

"Quite well," replied Xeala in a tone that barely concealed her surprise at her own words, "he has been really supportive of me through this whole process of pursuing the civil service exams, and has not tried to butt in or interfere with anything I do."

Xeala had not been the luckiest when it came to romantic liaisons. After some hurdles in her youth, Xeala had developed an unfortunate martyr like tendency to cut and run from relationships at the first sign of trouble, like pulling the rip cord too early on a parachute. Thankfully her present boyfriend, Axxen, was a gem of a person who was patient with her. He was extremely caring, he prioritized her and he was always there for her.

"Axxen was in town last weekend. We stayed in, we relaxed and had a great time. Oh, and we also found a Lo Scoglio outlet a few kilometers away from my place! And I finally had Nutella waffles after so long!" Xeala squealed excitedly.

"You are a sadistic person, do you know that?" I said, "I am going to die at forty of diabetes with both my feet cut off because of you. Thanks for introducing me to Lo Scoglio." I said with a hint of sarcasm in my voice.

"And the award for ungrateful asshole of the year goes to..." Xeala made the sound of a drum roll, "congratulations man! Take a bow."

I made a sniffing sound and said, "Thank you thank you! This had been my dream ever since I was a little boy. It has finally come true. To all the people of entitlement out there, I say, hang on, your time will come one day."

"Yeah right. Anyway, I have to go now, Axxen has been trying to get a hold of me on the phone for some time."

"Cool, I will speak to you later." I said and then hung up the phone.

Lo Scoglio was chain of cafes, that served amazing waffles and coffee. Their warm crispy waffles drenched in the topping of your choice were heavenly. There were many varieties to choose from, like Nutella, Ferrero Rocher, After Eight and Rocky Road. Each divine flavor provided a sublime sensory experience. The only event in my mind that compares with having your first Lo Scoglio waffle, is the first time you listen to 'Stairway To Heaven'. Their coffee, both the hot latte and cold brew variants, were amazing as well; thick, creamy and full of flavor. Fortunately for me, an outlet was located barely a few hundred meters from the place that I was renting in the city and whenever I had sweet cravings, I went there and indulged myself.

It was Xeala who had introduced me to Lo Scoglio, a place that she had discovered in her pursuit to find her favorite comfort food; Nutella waffles. It was there that she had taken me to let me know that she would be leaving. I personally think that there is nothing better than waffles that you can have on the table while breaking a terrifying or sad news to someone. If I am ever diagnosed with cancer, I would want my doctor to take me someplace that serves waffles and give me the news.

Talking about Lo Scoglio with Xeala had made me hungry. I decided to make the laborious effort of stepping out of my place and going waffle hunting. I was in the mood to try something new. Maybe I could go for the chocolate and cheese one.

PART 4: THE HEAVENS IN MOTION

I was fortunate to be working in a city that had a coastal location and the sea was barely a few kilometers away from my office. On days when I could get out of the office early, I often walked to the seaside, sat on one of the concrete benches that had been constructed on the well paved footpaths and looked out at the sea for hours on end. The benches were generous contributions of the deceased wealthy residents of the city, who sought to immortalize themselves by having their names embedded in marble plaques on the concrete seats.

It is quite remarkable how contemplative the sea makes me. As I sat there, I was vaguely aware of things happening in my periphery, of children screaming in excitement, of fitness enthusiasts and runners making the most of cool evenings, of vendors hawking their fares that ranged from plastic toys to masala tea to corn cobs and fritters, and of elderly gentlemen on their evening strolls in large groups, discussing politics and sports. Despite the assorted cacophony, my sole focus remained on the rolling waves dashing against the boulders of reclaimed land, chipping away at it, bit by bit. I became lost in the sea's immensity and expanse, and at times overwhelmed with the realization that I was looking at the source of all life on the planet.

The city was polluted. Probably we had all gotten accustomed to it and stopped noticing it, but it became evident when I went to the seaside on late evenings, hoping to catch a glimpse of the setting sun over the sea on the horizon. On most days the sky was too hazy to provide a clear view of the sun. The star got lost behind the clouds of noxious vapors even before it could make its way to the horizon. The heavens found it tough to compete with our maniacal tendency to make the planet's air unbreathable.

By this time, I was two years into my job, and it was starting to take its toll. I was not eating right, I did not have a fixed sleeping cycle, and I was unable to manage and separate my personal life from my professional life. I barely slept for five hours a day. There were times when I had to work with seniors who could not handle the stress themselves and let it percolate down to me, which did not help either. Things got really weird, when one morning, after an especially grueling time in the office the day before, I woke up from my sleep, and the first thing in my head was Alice Cooper's song, 'Welcome to my Nightmare'. In a meta fashion, that was the wakeup call I needed. I realized that it was time to stop doing something that I did not find any interest or joy in, and that I should try and do something that I would actually love. I took some time off, egged on by my boss, gave the matter a lot of thought, assessed my interests, and realized that I could pursue intellectual property rights law as a practice area. In my personal assessment, the practice area, by its nature, was more law oriented and less commerce oriented. It would allow me to develop my analytical skills as a lawyer and help me express my creativity while preparing legal drafts, rather than forcing me to become the jack of all trades, a role that I was clearly not adept at playing. Along with such an epiphany also came the realization that I was lucky to have the luxury to explore my options, because of my parents and because of the sacrifices they had made, working hard at their jobs, which they probably did not like themselves, to ensure that I would not be trapped in the same cycle as them. It was a humbling realization.

After a decision had been made, I communicated my intentions to my colleagues and seniors in the office and sorted out the paperwork which would allow me to bid adieu to my job. I was treated to a chocolate cake at my official farewell, made to order by Basuretta, who was aware of my fondness for the flavor. This was followed by a party at a pub called 'The Barking Deer', which was the venue for a more informal and unofficial farewell. It was with a bittersweet feeling that I was leaving the office. On the one hand I was free to pursue my interests and do something that I might actually enjoy, and on the other hand I was feeling wistful, since it was my first job after all. I was also lucky to have met some great people, and as well as to have made some incredible friends. Like most people at a crossroad in their lives, I started looking at everything through graduation goggles, fondly reminiscing about hardships and difficult times. I realized that, in a strange way, I would be missing the long hours, the heated discussions with colleagues, the insanity inducing demands from clients and most of all, ordering greasy food from the premier restaurants in town, because our clients, with their deep pockets, were footing the bill.

Eventually I conveyed the news of my departure to my friends outside office, including Xeala and Sandxira. I told them that I was planning to go back to my home city as I felt that opportunities would be plentiful and easier to come across for starting out in the intellectual property rights practice. Xeala was ecstatic and congratulated me heartily on my decision, even though by this time Xeala herself was getting a little stressed, because her civil service pursuits were not going as she had planned. I nevertheless felt blessed to have her encouragement.

Sandxira was quite supportive as well and said that she looked forward to meeting me when I came back home.

I did not leave for my home city immediately, but stayed back for a few days in the work city. I finally had time to explore the place and try finding the elusive sunset over the horizon that I had been searching for, which continued to evade me. In my pursuit I travelled out of the city whenever I could find the time. I researched on beaches and coastal places on the internet, got up on the local trains and travelled ten, fifteen, twenty stations out of the city to the very outskirts. Nearly all the trains stations were situated parallel to the coast and my destinations were easily accessible, once I got down at the stations.

My quest had brought me to some really amazing beaches. There was the rocky Manori beach, where a fort had been built right on the sea, but the sea had steadily and methodically smashed the fort to pieces, and had left behind chunks of ancient boulders, that once constituted the fort, on the beach. The beach itself looked like something right out of the pages of a medieval fantasy novel. To the right side of the beach was a raised plateau that stretched out for kilometers from the land out onto the sea and then plunged downwards into the water in a steep incline. It looked like the sleeping form of an immense green deity, who could wake up at any moment upon hearing the ancient music of the aboriginal Dreamtime. There was Gorai beach, that had a tiny film of water spread across its surface. The beach was one of the broadest that I had seen and the average width of it was nearly a kilometer. Hermit crabs frolicked in the shallow waters of the beach. In the evening sun, the beach looked like it was a mirror to the sky. The most remarkable of all these places was Madh beach, which was a long expanse of greyish black sand. I happened to visit the place on an overcast day and the entire place bore an ominous appearance, like it was the bridge between our realm and the dark gothic realm of the afterlife.

Despite my travels, my sunset continued to elude me.

It was finally when I was about to give up and surrender myself to the will of the universe, that I found myself walking to Dahanu beach during one of my last days in the city. I was near a fishing village and there was an accompanying slight stench of putrid fish in the air. I came across a wide coastal concrete embankment large enough for cars to be parked on. The embankment was at a slight elevation from the coast and formed a wall holding back the raging waves. I walked to the edge of the embankment and plopped myself down on the concrete, my legs folded under me. I looked out at the sea, waiting for the sun to dip.

As the seconds passed, the sun started making its way towards the horizon. At that moment I became acutely aware of how much we take our fragile existence for granted. It was by some incomprehensible happy co-incidence that our yellow star was situated at the exact distance from us that allowed life to flourish on this tiny blue planet. If the giant ball of exploding helium was to shift even a meter in either direction from its pre-determined orbit around the galaxy, life as we know on our planet would cease to exist. We would either be burnt to a crisp in a fiery inferno, as we struggled to breathe in a lost atmosphere, or be frozen stiff in a bizarre and painful diorama, as the planet covered itself in ice.

I began hoping that the setting sun would not be occluded by any clouds as it neared the horizon. This was my last chance.

By some unknown benevolence, the sun continued its journey towards the horizon uninterrupted, till its bottom touched the surface of the sea. From then on, the water rose to the star's middle, went up to its neck, till the final glorious moment arrived when the sun gave out a brief flicker of bright greenish light before being submerged in the depths of the sea, waiting to rise anew the next day. I briefly imagined the great god Ra dragging the sun behind him, the heavenly body chained to his divine barge as he made his way to the underworld, while preparing himself to fight off the ancient cosmic beast Apophis and its nightly attacks on the planet to consume all of Ra's creation.

I sat there, ecstasy coursing through my veins at the fantastic sight in front of me. At that moment, for some reason, the image of Sandxira came into my mind. I could not think of anyone else that I wanted to share that moment with more, than with her. It seemed like a whisper from a cosmic consciousness, whose existence I was agnostic about, telling me that I was meant to have Sandxira by my side and share with her the inimitable joy that comes from viewing the perfect sunset.

If the cosmic consciousness was keeping score, it probably had briefly gained a devotee that day.

PART 5: A CHANGE OF SCENERY

Deep down I knew that my habit of smoking was a psychological compulsion. It was not like smoking helped me think better, cleared my head, or even, as is the case with some people, made it a more seamless experience on the toilet in the morning. I had a feeling that when the stress of my present job would be over, it would be possible for me to stop the habit. So, on the night of my farewell party, I smoked my last cancer stick till date, and decided to give up the habit from the next day. When I woke up the following morning, I found it surprisingly easy to not fall back into the old habit. Something deep inside me had changed, some weight had been lifted, and I did not feel the compulsion to light a cigarette again.

A substantial portion of my earthly possessions, that I had acquired during my job, was books. More than actually having a desire to read the inordinate number of books, I had an unsettling compulsion to buy them, especially when coming across great deals on e-commerce websites. I was not a collector of books in the strictest sense. Collectors tend to preserve books in pristine mint conditions, without ever reading them, because such untainted and untouched copies are always worth a fortune. They are, after all, rare copies, which are highly valued. I was a hoarder. I was not precious about books and did not lust after first editions or signed author copies. Most of the times I bought paperbacks. I was a bit catholic about my tastes though, preferring science fiction, horror, noir, and thriller genres over all else. Till date I do not understand why paperbacks are considered by purists to be lesser forms of literature. They contain good stories, compelling characters and a lot of emotional depth. Some of my favorite authors like Isaac Asimov, Ray Bradbury and H.P. Lovecraft had made their mark in paperbacks. We can't all be reading 'War and Peace', or the title that the book was originally supposed to be published under, 'War, What Is It Good For'.

Every time I walked past a bookstore, I had to pretend that I was wearing blinkers. Things were not helped with a secondhand bookstore having set up shop very close to my rented place. Consequently, when I ended up packing my belongings and shipping them home, I packed a hundred kilo of books. I had five boxes in which to pack my belongings, and nearly four of them were filled with books.

Close to three weeks after my last day in office, I arrived back home. **Sandxira** and I had planned to catch up for a walk and dinner after I got back. It was her suggestion.

She had reached just in time at the Jadavpur bus terminus which I had suggested as the meeting point. I had barely managed to reach the place a few minutes before her, and stood at the bus terminus trying to avoid the oncoming crowds of people, who were herding themselves like lemmings from one destination to the next. I was waving my hand in front of my face to dissipate the partially combusted diesel fumes of buses trudging out of the terminus, like ancient groaning mechanical whales. Suddenly my phone buzzed and looking into it, I saw that it was a message from Sandxira asking me where I was. Following the descriptions of her whereabouts, I walked towards the place where she said that she was standing, and I spotted her. She saw me and waved. I crossed a narrow road and stood next to her. We awkwardly shook hands. I was meeting Sandxira after a long time and neither of us were sure of the permissible protocol on physical contact, when two people, who were a little more than work proximity associates, were meeting each other after a year.

Sandxira looked stunning, yet there was no alchemy involved in the process. She was dressed simply and had no make-up on. She wore a grey sundress with black vertical stripes and open toed sandals on her feet. Her hair looked freshly washed and as usual it was still curly and bunched over her right shoulder. In a casual, elegant yet simple way, she looked resplendent.

"Hi!" she said brightly.

"Hey! How have you been? It is so nice to see you." I said.

"I am good! How have you been?"

"Doing well. I just got back a few days ago."

"Oh great." she said.

Clearly a fair amount of ice had formed once again between us and it would be some time before conversation could really sparkle. To an outsider, it looked like we were reading to each other from a script written by an unimaginative screenwriter.

"Thanks for meeting me here," she continued, "I have never been to this part of the city. It is quite far away from my home here."

"No problem," I said, "it was easier for me to reach here as well. It is barely a couple of kilometers from my place. It is not much, but this Jadavpur area is like a one stop shop for all your marketing needs. Kind of an early version of a shopping mall, except all the shops are spread out over a larger area and instead of air conditioning, you get to enjoy the natural elements like sweltering heat and rainfall while browsing for your shopping requirements."

"Oh really?" her enthusiasm did not seem superficial.

"You have shops for everything, ranging from sporting goods, clothes, fruit sellers, tea shops, fast food joints, grocery stores to even photocopy shops and bookstores." I said.

"You sound like a shopkeeper yourself, rolling off the names of so many goods and services in one breathless sentence." she observed with a playful smile.

"Just pitching the virtues of this place to you, since you have never been here." I said and shrugged, "You must have seen places like these before, right?"

"I have, yes. The crowd is quite familiar. Reminds me of this place in our earlier city. That place was always bustling too. Do you remember its name?"

"You mean Dadar?" I said.

"Yes," she said, "that is the one." she confirmed.

"Don't I know that," I said, "I used to walk through the Dadar market place every day to reach the train station and take the train to office. It was probably the only stretch of road that made me mortally afraid to listen to music and become oblivious to the world around me, while walking. There was always a risk of being run over by a car or being trampled in an ill-timed stampede."

Sandxira laughed lightly.

"However, this place has a strange and quaint charm." she conceded.

"That is does." I acknowledged, "it's oddly calming and therapeutic for a lot of folks. In addition, there is immense scope to haggle with shopkeepers over prices. Something about it makes people feel alive."

She beamed again.

We had stepped out of the bus terminus and were walking along the side of the main road that was facing oncoming traffic. Shops had taken over the sidewalk and there was no space for two persons to be able to walk comfortably, next to each other. The road was brightly lit in places with sodium vapor lamps, and at other places, the brighter LED lights from the shops had established dominance over the street lights. As we walked on the road, Sandxira's face occasionally lit up with a yellowish hue.

I had grown out my beard over the past few months, before returning home and had decided upon the lumberjack being my signature look for the foreseeable future. Thanks to my dwarfish genes, I was able to grow a full beard unlike a lot of other men of my ilk, for whom beards come out patchy. By dwarfish, I refer to dwarves of Tolkienian fantasy fiction, who are so shaggy that hair does not serve as a gender distinction for them. Fun fact about dwarves, they use a singular pronoun to indicate all sexes. All dwarves have ferocious beards. Gender is more or less optional for them.

"I see the beard is new." Sandxira said.

Without conscious effort and almost reflexively, I raised my hand and stroked my facial hair.

"Are you planning to become a model for one of the men's grooming product brands?" she teased, "because you know, I can hook you up. The company I am working for, is coming up with products of its own to compete in this booming market."

"Nothing like that." I smiled, "although I would not mind getting a piece of that lucrative proverbial pie. The fact is I gained quite a bit of weight over these past couple of years, so I thought that growing out the beard will make my face look slightly thinner. Cover up the multiple chins, the bulging cheeks and what not. You know how it was at work right? Toiling for long hours, barely having any weekends off, and even when I did get free weekends, I just wanted to lie down and decompress, instead of exercising or going somewhere."

"Yeah, I know what you mean. It was one of the reasons I wanted to move out of there. I had already had my fill of the work experience in such a law firm. I did not feel that there was anything new which the place could offer." Sandxira said.

"Yup. It is hard to believe now that 1 a.m., almost every night, was a normal time to get out of office. Christmas came early on days when we got to leave at 11 p.m. It was a really strange time." I said.

"I remember being staffed on a transaction that was to be closed in one week," she said, "when the normal time period for such deals to close is one month. We nearly died those seven days, metaphorically speaking of course."

"I know! Last year, towards the end, for some reason, the financial markets had really slowed down, and we barely had any live transactions at work. Every day we left office at 7 p.m. It was one of those, rare stars being favorably aligned, situations. We had inadvertently traded in every good karma that we had earned in our lives, for the sweet sweet early release from work."

"I know what you mean."

"Yeah..." I sighed wistfully, having fished out the graduation goggles from my back pocket and put them on.

"So, is that the reason why you left the job?" Sandxira asked.

By this time, we had walked on to the university campus that was close by, and we went inside. The campus, being situated right in the middle of the city, was usually accessible to regular people, who were not students. Of course, when it had been established close to a hundred years ago, the university campus was quite far away from the main city. A person had to trek through arid deserts, bargain with djinns, trudge through rainforests, fight off dragons, slay succubi and answer riddles by Sphinxes before reaching the university gates. However, over the years, the city had gradually expanded and grew around the university campus, and much like The Thing from outer space, had assimilated the university as a part of itself.

There were several ponds inside the campus, and nearly all of them had recently had their embankments reinforced with concrete. The university was the favorite haunt of young broke lovers, looking to have romantic experiences without burning holes in their pockets or awkwardly asking their parents for money to fund their liaisons. The campus did have its charms. It seemed like the whole place was covered in a massive glass dome that cut off all the noise from the outside world, once we stepped inside the premises. We only had to be careful of junkies huddled in dark unillumi-nated corners sniffing glue or finding solace in some other narcotic to get their next high, but they were more afraid of us than we could ever be of them. The junkies were quite harmless, but it always made for a disconcerting experience to cross paths with them, tripping about in their altered states of consciousness.

We walked under the shadow of a massive banyan tree. Through the leaves of the behemoth, slivers of yellow street light passed through, like numerous overlapping double slit experiments. I said to Sandxira "That was one of the reasons that I had to leave yes, but frankly I was not enjoying the work there, and when that happens, everything you do becomes a chore. It makes it harder to put up with the pressure. It was kind of an abusive relationship to be honest."

"That bad, huh?" she seemed sympathetic.

"I spoke to my boss a few months before I left. I was really fortunate to have one as considerate and understanding as he was. I told him that I would prefer to work in some other area of practice. He told me that it never sets a good example. People in office tend to look at you differently. They presume you are an opportunist, a foot in the door kind of a person, that you just agreed to join your present practice area as a way to get into the firm, and then use the opportunity to try and worm your way into another practice, instead of sticking it out in the one for which you have been hired in the first place." I explained.

"That is harsh." Sandxira observed.

"Yeah, it was and it was an eye opener too. I figured that the window was closing in on me to reboot my life and start working on something that I could actually love. I am quite sure that if I had continued any longer, I would have been stuck in the role of a capital markets lawyer for the rest of my career, whether I liked it or not. I mean, it has got a nice ring to it, if I am being honest, makes me feel all hoity toity, but it is not really all that it is built up to be."

"I see. I remember that you had told me that you wanted to pursue a career in intellectual property rights law, right?" Sandxira reminded me.

"Yes, I did," I confirmed, "I feel that it is the only practice area that made sense to me, and which had some logic to it. Law has always been a sort of arranged marriage for me. It was never my first choice. Maybe subconsciously I had always resisted the subjects that were taught to me in law school, but when I studied intellectual property rights law, I fell in love with it. It was something familiar. I had pursued science papers in my board exams and most of the law papers and their open-ended interpretation sounded like gibberish to me. That was probably the reason why I latched onto intellectual property rights law because it had logic and structure, or at least that was the way I felt."

"Oh wow! It is rare to meet someone who truly knows where their interests lie, as it is with you. Most people take much longer to figure things out." she said in a complimentary tone.

I blushed, but thankfully my reddening cheeks were invisible in the intermittent darkness. In the most falsely modest tone that I could muster, I said, "I feel that is it a good place for a fresh start."

Sandxira looked at me and smiled again. She looked radiant.

As a kid, whenever I travelled anywhere, mostly on long train journeys, I had a preference to sit on the right side of the train, facing the direction in which the train was travelling. The left side seemed to be cold, distant and uninviting like a foster family which is forced to take care of you and provide you with sustenance but which never really cares for you. The right-side exuded warmth, compassion, comfort, familiarity and understanding. It was a lot more daydream worthy, and I would lose myself in my fantasies, a lot of which, during my growing up years, were about serenading a person I was romantically interested in, in the valleys, fields and mountains that were visible from the right side of the train. Looking at Sandxira right then, for some reason the memories of such train journeys and of the daydreams were evoked in me. They reminded me of a simpler time, and filled me with incredible wistfulness and nostalgia.

"Here I am going on about myself." I said, "Tell me, how have you been doing? How has your work been? And I belatedly apologize for subjecting you to my pity rant."

"Oh no! You are being needlessly modest." Sandxira assured me, "It has honestly been great meeting you after so long. I am glad to see a familiar face. I have been quite well and work has been good too. The great thing about working in a company like this, is that even though I have a lot of deliverables, I can plan it according to my schedule and there is no one to micromanage me. So, at present I am working on the company's portfolio of cigarettes, and mainly handling compliance work in relation to them. It is one of the company's busiest portfolios, but I am never dying with work here, metaphorically speaking again. I get to have a balanced personal and professional life. This is a slow city anyway and there is not much you can do after you leave office in terms of having an active social life. I am not a fan of any of my co-workers to be honest, but at least I have the option of leaving office at a reasonable hour or even earlier if I want to, and carry on work from home."

"Wow! That does sound great."

As I said this, we arrived at a small stall that sold cigarettes, biscuits, chips and cold drinks; stuff that students need to survive in college, especially during long study nights before examinations, when they are trying to stay awake and cram in chapters and class notes. A variety of biscuits were stacked on two shelves, that were arranged perpendicular to each other, such as butter flavored biscuits, chocolate chip biscuits, pistachio biscuits, salted biscuits, and even underrated and under-appreciated, Marie biscuits. Tied to a corner of the shop were two hanger-like contraptions, passing through which were long chains of bite sized snack food packets such as cakes and chips. The feathery light packets were swinging in the mild evening breeze. The proprietor of the shop, a dark middle-aged man with greying hair and a pot belly, was hooked onto his mobile phone. Both his earphones were plugged in and he was watching videos on it. His desire to watch videos on his phone had triumphed over any ambition he had of running his business. The man was sitting with his back to the third wall of the shop. In front of him was a big tray on which cigarettes packets were stacked tightly, like sardines in a tin. It appeared that business had not been great that day, or it could be possible that the proprietor had a secret stash of more cigarettes hidden away somewhere else, from which he replenished the tray in front of him when it periodically emptied.

Sandxira turned to me, an anticipatory gaze in her eyes. It took a moment for me to register what she was expecting me to do.

"Oh! Oh sorry! I forgot to tell you. I have stopped smoking." I said with a light laugh.

"What?! That is amazing! How did you give up?" Sandxira asked.

"I don't know," I shrugged, "I think I realized that the habit was completely psycho-somatic, but despite the realization, I continued to use smoking as a crutch as long as I worked in that office. So, on my last day I smoked my final cigarette and then was done. Went cold turkey. Was not that difficult surprisingly."

"I am so proud of you" she said, patting me on the hand in appreciation.

"Thanks," I said, "you are too kind. It was awfully sweet of you to bring me here."

"Not a problem," she laughed, "Although I am sorry to have lost one of our most loyal customers. In fact, right at this moment, one of my drawers at work is full of cigarettes packets of some new flavors. The designs on them require customs clear-ance."

"Oh really?" I asked, "what flavors?"

"There is a lime one, a strawberry one and a chocolate one. Whoever did the market research for the company before coming out with the flavors is either incompetent or is attempting some big prank and hoping to get away with it."

I laughed heartily. Of all the weirdest cigarette flavors that anyone could have thought of, chocolate was surely on the top of that list.

"Anyway," said Sandxira, "the cigarettes are not in the market yet. I could have gifted you some as a homecoming present, you know, an exclusive peek" she sighed, "Thank you for smoking." she gave me a mock salute.

"Thank you for your consideration." I said, "The flavors sound egregious and outrageous, but I honestly would not have minded trying out the chocolate one."

Sandxira smiled sadly and shrugged.

We decided that it was time for us to pick a place to eat. The good thing about Jadavpur was that there were lots of options for everyone. The eateries ranged from places that charged pre-independence prices, but served enough food to fill you up, to those which were so expensive that you would end up paying the bill in monthly instalments, unless you were the beneficiary of a trust fund. I was really at a loss trying to figure out where to take Sandxira. I did not want to go someplace too cheap, or come off as pretentious by going someplace too expensive. I had to hit that sweet spot in between. With growing dread, I realized that I should have paid more attention when I had come to Jadavpur all those times before, and scoped out restaurants for eventualities like these. The choice was becoming more difficult to make as the minutes passed, because I was gradually becoming famished, and the enticing aroma of food wafting in from various eateries, with their different cuisines, were confusing and overwhelming me. It was a relief when Sandxira tugged at my T-shirt sleeve and said, "Hey! What about the Big Kahuna over there?" She was pointing a few meters ahead of us. "That restaurant looks good." she said.

We walked towards the establishment. As we reached closer, I went a couple of steps ahead of Sandxira, pulled open the door of the restaurant and gestured for her to precede me into the air-conditioned interior. A waiter approached us at once and showed us to a table that had just been vacated. The place was doing good business. The crowd consisted mainly of families. The squeals of little children who were enjoying a special restaurant meal with their parents and siblings, rang in the air. The place was lit with blue lights. A few multi colored balloons were still taped to some of

the pillars. Evidently, the place had recently been rented out for some sort of cele-
bratory event, probably a birthday party. The management had decided to let the
balloons be, probably because it lent the place a more festive look.

We sat down at a table for four. The restaurant was probably not expecting too many
patrons, since closing was only an hour away. The waiter smiled as he handed both
of us individual menu cards. The restaurant was a multi-cuisine one and the menu
was filled with names of generic dishes that a thousand other restaurants served all
over the country. The prices, however, were reasonable and the place seemed to hit
that sweet spot that I was looking for, between not being too expensive and not being
too cheap either.

Studying the menu, I decided to let Sandxira order.

"See something appetizing?" I asked.

"Trying to figure it out. Do you have any preferences?" asked Sandxira.

"Not really, except for..." I proceeded to list out a few food items that I was allergic
to.

The waiter had returned with a pen and notepad, and was standing next to our table
expectantly. I looked at him closely and was comforted to see that he looked like
someone whom I would not mind handling my food. I was not an elitist; it was simply
a pet peeve of mine, unwittingly imbibed, after having seen Tyler Durden being *the*
guerilla terrorist of the food service industry, in 'Fight Club'.

"Are you ready to order?" he asked.

"Waiting for the lady to decide. Could you give us a couple of minutes?" I said softly.

"Sure," and saying so, the waiter walked away.

"Is there anything on the menu that seems interesting?" I asked Sandxira again.

"Hmm…" she replied, as if lost in deep contemplation.

I waited for some time, focusing my attention on the design notched near the rim of the ceramic plate in front of me, trying to find out if any secret pattern would emerge from it. Sandxira flipped the menu over to the other side in the intervening period. When adequate time had passed, and I figured that Sandxira would have thoroughly read through the entire menu at least once, like an auditor going through the financial papers of a company, I asked her "So, are you planning to stay in your present job for some time?"

"I am not sure about it" she replied, "it has only been a year since I joined here, but I do not see myself continuing in this place for a long time."

"Is something wrong with the work culture?"

"Not really. Like I said, the profile is good and I work with tolerable people, but the work experience that I was after is close to being fulfilled."

"Is that something you tend to do? Shift from place to place, picking up nuggets of experience? How do you know if you even like something if you do not stick to it for a long term?" I asked in an impish tone.

"You figured out in two years that you do not like capital markets." Sandxira said, her eyes still scanning the menu.

"Fair enough" I said sheepishly, while mentally picturing myself consulting a podiatrist to extract the foot that was lodged in my mouth.

Sandxira looked up at the tone of my voice and smiled placatingly.

"It's just that I have some engagements planned up ahead that I need to take care of, which would require a change of place and may require me to move out of this city. So, let us see how things pan out."

Saying so, she signaled at the waiter who approached eagerly to take down our order.

I felt a little deflated and discouraged when she told me that she might be moving soon. It was not like I had built up elaborate notions in my head about a relationship with Sandxira, but now that both of us were in the same city, I had held out hope that I would be seeing a lot more of her and maybe get a chance to know her better. But it was probably not to be. The theme music of Father's Funeral from Hellboy started playing in my head.

I must have inadvertently let my thoughts be expressed on my face. Sandxira suddenly reached out and placed her hand on mine. She said, "I am sorry if this is upsetting you."

"Oh no! Not at all. I am not a kid," I hurried to cover up, "it just brought back some difficult memories. Do you remember Xeala? She used to work with us in our earlier firm. She was one of my close friends in the old work place."

"Yes, I think I have met her a few times." Sandxira said.

"I think you did, yes. It's just that she too decided to quit her job and pursue civil service examinations. When she left, I took it quite hard. It was a difficult life in the office, and she made all of it tolerable. She was always there to cheer me up, and she also gave me the best birthday party that I could have hope for, especially when I was away from home. Then suddenly one day she told me that she had decided to leave. It felt like I had lost my anchor and was left adrift. I know that you and I do not know each other that well, but I was hoping we could have changed that, since both of us were supposed to be in the same city." I said, letting out a sigh.

Sandxira squeezed my hand a little harder. She said, "Let's see if we can do that, in the coming few months."

I smiled and simply looked back at her.

"So, tell me some more things about Xeala. She sounds like a special person." Sandxira said.

"Yes, she truly is," I said, and proceeded to tell her stories about our shenanigans, of trying to go out ritualistically for drinks on Friday nights, of grooving to the shared taste of classic rock music, of cruising around in the city in a taxi in the dead of the night, wind blowing in our hairs, of walking by the sea coast, talking about life, the universe and everything. I also told her the story of the one time that Xeala and I had surreptitiously trespassed into someone's sea facing home and climbed up to their terrace. We had sat on the terrace for a long time looking out at the sea. The waves were crashing onto the boulders far below, and the distant light of passing ships were visible on the horizon. Sandxira sat with her elbows on the table, her closed palms holding up her face. Her eyes were animated and she was smiling as she heard my stories.

We sat there talking, waiting for our food to arrive. I realized that by concentrating on her words, I had an excuse for staring at her face. Soon the waiter came back, carrying a tray with the food that we had ordered for our table.

"Oh great! Food is here, I am starving." Sandxira said.

"As am I." I said and struggled with opening the tightly knotted napkin that had been placed on the right side of my plate, so that I could extricate the knife, fork and spoon that had been bundled inside like a swaddled newborn baby. Sandxira proceeded to do the same and in the process dropped a knife that cluttered to the floor with a resounding clang. The tables around us went momentarily quiet. She closed her eyes tightly at the sound and then slowly opened them grinning at me apologetically. The waiter promptly proceeded to replace the knife.

Looking at the food, the whole knife dropping incident seemed pointless. There was no item on the table that would require the use of a knife to eat it.

"Bon Appetit" she said, and both of us proceeded to dig in.

Sure, there was no need for a knife, but a new opportunity for me to make a fool of myself and bring balance to the Force, presently came along. In addition to the knife, fork and spoon, I noticed that a pair of chopsticks had been wrapped up in paper covering and left standing next to the tray of condiments that contained tiny covered bowls of garlic sauce, soya sauce and chilies in vinegar. Despite lacking the necessary skills to be able to use chopsticks, I picked them up anyway and fiddled with them. I realized soon that it was the wrong night to show off. I found myself unable to pick up a noodle or a slice of chicken without the thing sliding out of my grasp and falling back with a plop where I had picked it up from. I felt my ears turning red and had to finally give up when in a final act of defiance, a piece of curried potato that I had managed to snag between the jaws of the chopsticks, slipped away from me. I watched in horror as the potato landed on the table cloth, splashed sauce across it and began skipping towards Sandxira. It was by some unknown intervention that close to the moment of impact, the piece of potato seemed to suddenly change direction, evaded its quarry, and landed with a dull thump on the floor, splashing a tiny bit of sauce on Sandxira's left foot before coming to rest.

"Well, that makes us even," Sandxira said smiling. She took a tissue paper from the table and wiped her foot.

I was mortified but relieved that Sandxira found the situation humorous.

"Maybe it is time to switch up the cutlery." she said.

"That is fair." I said, "My co-ordination is all messed up"

She smiled in understanding.

We continued to eat, momentarily focused on the food, as I tried to navigate the spoon to ensure that food did not get smeared on my beard. The effort was fairly successful. Sandxira had looked up and laughed at me only once when she saw my paleolithic eating habits. She spotted some curry on my beard and handed me a tissue to wipe it off.

"That reminds me," I said, "it is an odd segue, and more for my curiosity than anything else, but why did you unhesitatingly turn me down, when I had asked out you nearly a year ago? You had said that we could address the proverbial elephant in the room, when we met back home."

She gulped down her bite, and then became silent for a while as she toyed with her food. The meat on her plate had developed a cold, gelatinous look.

"I thought that I would not need to give you any explanations and we would eventually forget about each other, that you would remain a footnote for me. The fact is, I am really enjoying your company tonight, a lot more than I expected to, if I am being honest," she said, "and that makes me scared, that when you learn what I have to tell you, you will not look at me the same way again. So, let me just enjoy this night with you. Let us just be in the moment. I promise that I will tell you soon, just not tonight. I hope you will be okay with that." Sandxira said.

"Of course!" I said, "we are friends. I am more than fine with it. If it makes you feel any better, you do not need to tell me at all. I understand that you must have your reasons and I respect them."

She reached out and squeezed my hand again.

"Besides, we need to fill the pages." I said.

"What's that?"

"Oh, it is just a joke. Like if you and I were characters in a book, the writer would need to put off the big revelation for a while, so that he could fill in the pages with the necessary build up."

Sandxira laughed.

"Do you like the food?" I asked.

"It is unexpectedly good. I was not hungry when we met but I have managed to work up quite an appetite during our walk."

When we finished eating, the waiter came back to clean away the dishes and plates.

"Would you like some dessert?" he asked.

I deferred Sandxira and she picked brownie with vanilla ice cream. Both of us were feeling quite full after our meal, so we decided to share the dessert more as a palate cleanser than having any actual craving for it. The waiter inclined his head forward in the most minimal bow and moved off, his arms heavy with crockery.

When dessert arrived, we both picked up spoons and began to chip away at the brownie, taking the smallest portion possible for ourselves out of some chivalrous obligation of leaving more for the other person. The vanilla ice cream melted steadily and pooled like a white moat around the brownie. In the end we decided that it was only fair that I get a larger share of the brownie, owing to my bigger bulk.

When the bill arrived, as men are wont to, I nearly pounced on it.

"I got this." I said,

"No no, let us share the bill." Sandxira insisted.

"Come on, let me get this, you can get the next one."

"Let me pay for half the bill," she said, "otherwise I will not feel comfortable hanging out with you in the future, if you insist on picking up entire bills like this."

After the minutest pause, I said, "Fair enough," and signaled to the waiter, who had relegated himself to a corner, after placing the bill gently on our table. He had been expectantly looking at us, as we sorted out our mild discord over who gets to pay the bill.

"We will split it equally." I told him.

"Very well Sir." said the waiter, and pulled out a card machine that he had kept hidden in his hands which were folded behind his back.

We paid the bill, grabbed a pinch of mouth freshening fennel each and stepped out of the restaurant. I turned back for a final glance to appreciate the Big Kahuna.

It had gotten late and a heavy breeze had started to blow, in anticipation of rain later in the night. The sky had turned a dull orangish color. The grey thunder clouds reflected the yellow street lights.

"Come on, I will get you a taxi." I said.

"Can I drop you somewhere? Would your home be enroute?" Sandxira asked.

"Nope. Unfortunately, you and I will be going in opposite directions, thanks for the offer though. I will make some arrangement for myself."

We walked to the taxi stand, where yellow Ambassador cars were parked in a row, waiting for fares. Next to the taxi stand was a wall with posters covering every available inch of it. The posters advertised myriad goods and services, like holistic medicines, English language tutorials, massages with happy endings, astrology consultations and repair services for electronic gadgets.

We found a taxi that agreed to take Sandxira to her home. She had packed up some extra food from the restaurant which she could not finish, and even I could not polish off. She opened the back door of the taxi, and placed the plastic packet with the food on the backseat. She hesitated for a moment with her left hand on the half open door. Then she turned around and hugged me with one hand across my shoulder and one hand across my back, her face digging into my left shoulder blade and her left breast pressed against my right chest. The hug lasted longer than I had expected. After a while, we finally broke apart. I was left pleasantly surprised, and shamefully realized that I had a barely concealed tumescence in my pants. I thanked myself for having decided to wear denim trousers that day.

Sandxira got into the taxi, poked her head out and said, "See you around," as the taxi came to life and let out a gust of exhaust. The taxi began pulling out of the stand and she called out saying, "I had a really great time! Thanks for tonight."

"Message me when you reach home." I shouted in turn, waving.

The taxi pulled out of parallel parking, got out onto the road and picked up speed. It left a cloud of fumes behind, with me silhouetted in their midst.

PART 6: HEAVY LUENTO

A few weeks later Sandxira and I found ourselves strolling on the riverside. Like nearly every other major city, this city too had come up along the banks of a river, that ran through the middle of the city, dividing it into residential and industrial areas. We were on the residential side of the river.

I was envious of Sandxira for having an incredibly well-located office. It was right in the middle of the financial district of the city. Despite the place being a hub for business and being the location of numerous other offices, it never felt crowded. The place was a testament to one of the few good things that had come out of being under the thumb of colonial rule for a few hundred years; well-planned architecture. The entire area had been established during the early days of the city. The buildings were well spaced out, the roads were quite wide, and major tourist sites of the city, like the museum, the planetarium, the botanical gardens and even the riverside were very conveniently located at short distances away. Cool windy evenings were ideal for a walk from Sandxira's office to any of these locations.

Located a couple of buildings away from Sandxira's office was one of the most important libraries in the city. The library itself was not massive in size, but had an extensive and excellent collection of international books and journals that were rare and were almost never to be found anywhere else. The library was only three storeys high, and each floor had an area of roughly three thousand square feet. The library catered to the widest of tastes; from sophisticated discourses that appealed to intelligentsia and academicians, to more accessible comic books and pulp literature that found favor with readers like me.

I had recently secured a new job in a law firm as an intellectual property rights lawyer. It was a much more relaxed work atmosphere, in comparison to my previous job. The office hours were better, there were no expectations for associates to work, or even be available for work on weekends, and the work itself was quite interesting, challenging and varied. I was enjoying myself, and could finally balance my personal and professional lives.

Every once in a while, the associates were required to come in to office on one of the days of the weekend, but we were allowed to leave immediately after lunch. The rest of the afternoon and evening were for ours to spend as we pleased. Sometimes, during those weekends, I went to the library. The place was open till 6 p.m. in the evening. After finding a place to myself at a corner table, I piled on books catering to my taste and devoured them. They were mostly comic books, or to use the politically correct term, graphic novels. For some reason they were incredibly expensive and I could never bring myself to spend a fortune on them, hoarder of books though I was. I relied on the library's extensive collection to get me through.

I had vaguely known that Sandxira's office was somewhere close to the library, but had somehow never tried to find out where it was exactly. It was a little like being afraid of checking your test scores online, choosing to find solace in ignorance. In addition, the memory of my evening and dinner with Sandxira was quite pleasant in my mind and I was apprehensive of having that memory sullied. I kept playing that previous night on a loop in my head, reliving the sequence of events again and again, afraid that I would stop remembering if I stopped thinking about them; our walk, her animated face, her smile, sitting down for dinner and her warm and intimate embrace.

For some reason I was seized with an unexplained compulsion. It was like something was overwhelming me, pressing down on my chest and forcing me to act. I realized that the only way to get rid of this compulsion and weight on me was by seeing Sandxira again.

It was a Saturday, one of those few occasions when I was required to be in office on the weekend, but could leave by lunch time and was free to make plans. I had planned to spend my evening at the library anyway, so I decided to check if Sandxira would be available to hang out. I messaged her on my way out from work, asking her how she was and how things were at her end.

My phone immediately lit up with a "Hi!".

We briefly texted, bringing each other up to speed about our lives. I told her about my new job and she congratulated me for having secured work in my preferred area of practice.

"So, I have some news as well," she messaged, "I have finally decided to quit this job. I think I have gained enough work experience. I am considering putting in my resignation in a couple of months."

"Oh..." I wrote back, "Are you leaving immediately after, then?"

"Actually, I have to serve two more months as my notice period and then I will be able to leave. So, four months in total." she clarified and summed up.

Cue Father's Funeral.

It is easy to mask one's emotions over text messages, as I had to do at that moment when I read her message. It seemed like a ticking clock had been set up with nothing, but emptiness at the end. In four months Sandxira would be gone from this city and I would become a mere footnote in her life. I let the entire theme of Father's Funeral play out in my head before I replied to her.

"Oh... I see," I wrote back, "Good for you."

It is easy to fake sincerity too.

"Any thoughts on what you intend to do after this?" I wrote further.

"I am planning to travel for some time, explore new places. I will figure it out as I go along." Sandxira replied.

Even though I could not sense her tone, her answer appeared to be guarded and vague. She was not inclined to reveal too much. I did not ask any further questions as I did not want to appear too intrusive.

"By the way, I am actually headed to," I mentioned the name of the library, "I think it is close to your office."

"Oh yes! It is a couple of buildings away. Will you be there for some time?" Sandxira's tone appeared eager.

"I was planning to be there for a couple of hours, maybe till 5."

"Great! I am in office today as well, have been called in for a few hours. Maybe we can catch up after 5 then?"

"That would be nice! Do you have a place in mind where we could go to?" I asked.

"How about I meet you and then we can figure it out?" she messaged back.

"Okay," I wrote, "looking forward to it."

The library complex had heavy security measures in place. The third storey had been recently added and housed an embassy. I had to pass through a set of magnetic lock enabled doors, and hand over my personal belongings, including my backpack, for screening. I passed through a metal detector, while my backpack got scanned and its embarrassing contents, such as a tube of anti-fungal cream, were revealed to the se-curity officer who inspecting my backpack through the x-ray machine. After passing through the metal detector, I was handed back my personal belongings, as well as a temporary visitor's pass for non-members of the library. I had to use the pass to open the next set of magnetic doors. Only then did I reach the actual library building.

The two hours that I had, between reaching the library and seeing Sandxira, were spent restlessly. Despite our last hang out having gone quite well, I felt nervous and apprehensive. I realized that in spite of my intentions not to do so, I had once again put Sandxira on a pedestal and was anxious that I could potentially embarrass myself in front of her by doing something ludicrous or saying something ridiculous.

I could barely concentrate on what I was reading and unmindfully read through the same comic panel at least five or six times. The comic was a 2000AD one, about Judge Death and his acolytes Judge Mortis, Judge Fear and Judge Fire coming back from the netherworld and infiltrating the physical plane, in order to extract revenge upon Judge Dredd, who had killed them and damned their souls.

The clock eventually struck five. I rose from my table but my feet felt oddly light and spongy. They were incapable of supporting my weight and would probably make me topple over. I managed to walk to the bathroom and tried to calm myself. I gave myself a pep talk in the mirror about not overthinking things. Sandxira was the one who asked me to meet her, which meant that she had actually thought about making plans with me, when she could have simply ignored me and gone on with her life. This meant that it was no longer my job to make her like me, it was my job not to mess it up.

Having succeeded in calming myself down, I got out of the library.

I had always thought that the phrase "a couple of buildings away" was a figure of speech and the actual distance between Sandxira's office and the library was probably more. I was pleasantly surprised, upon checking my phone, to find out that I would be arriving at my destination in half a minute, despite travelling on foot.

I walked to the front of the building and sat down on a bench at a bus stop that was close by. I messaged Sandxira saying that I had arrived. She replied shortly afterwards saying that she would take ten more minutes to reach.

I took out a set of earphones from my pocket and plugged it into my phone. Then I opened the music app and started scrolling through the heavy metal anthems on my phone, before selecting one and hitting play.

I have always favored the heavy metal genre since college. Before my first year, I had never been knowledgeable, passionate or even precious about music. I usually listened to what was available and did not have any preferences. Worst of all, I was very impatient and had a short attention span when it came to music. However, all this changed in my second year in college when I discovered heavy metal music. Hallucinogens may have had a small role to play in it as well, by altering the constitution of my mind, and making me much more patient and appreciative of music, especially the poetry of the heavy metal genre.

As the song was coming to a close, I felt a tap on my shoulder. Earphones still plugged in, I turned around to see Sandxira standing behind me smiling, In the process of hurriedly standing up to greet her, my left earphone popped out and began swinging like a pendulum. I quickly grabbed it and brought it to a halt.

"Hi", she said smiling, and proceeded to hug me. This time it felt more formal and perfunctory, with only her right arm around my neck. Her left hand was still by her side and her body was arched away from me.

"Have you been waiting for a long time?" she asked.

"I do not think so. Might be around eight minutes I guess?"

"That is oddly precise."

I laughed. "Not really. Master of Puppets is a little over eight minutes long. I started listening to it when I sat down and it just got over so..." I raised my shoulders in a halfhearted shrug.

By this time, we were standing on the side of the road, waiting for the traffic signal to turn red so that we could cross to the other side. That day she was wearing black trousers and a sap green sweater. Slivers of the white blouse that she was wearing underneath were peeking out from her collar and from the bottom of her sweater.

"I see." Sandxira said.

I thought that would be the end of it, a polite acknowledgement from her.

"What is the song about?" I was surprised to hear her follow-up question.

"Well, it is about addiction," I said, "mainly addiction to cocaine in the context of the song, but it is universally applicable to addiction of all sorts - can be alcohol, heroin, synthetic drugs, or even something as widely prevalent but woefully ignored like food addiction. The song is about how an addiction can be so ruthless, overwhelming and all-encompassing that it takes up every aspect of your life and all you are left with are broken dreams. The goal of your life becomes looking for the next hit. The song is about how the substance that you are abusing, ends up abusing and killing you."

"That is very poignant. You seem to have done substantial introspection on this song." Sandxira said. I could not figure if her praise was patronizing or genuine.

"I did, yes. It was kind of my go to song, every time I was out on the balcony in our last office, smoking. But I feel that this song has an alternate meaning as well. It is not only about addiction in the form of substance abuse, but also about the psychological barriers that we place on ourselves, by staying confined to our comfort zone, which makes us complacent and lulls us into a false sense of happiness and contentment. Complacency prevents us from going for what we want."

"I agree." she said and slipped her hand into my hand. I fought my momentary instinct to pull my hand away, and closed my palm around hers. I could feel the color rising in my cheeks.

We had to walk a kilometer to get to the riverside. This part of the city used to be the mainstay of the colonists a hundred years ago. There were huge lush green grounds with grass that was neatly trimmed. In the evening one would find families sitting on the grounds, enjoying a cool breeze that blew in from the river. Children could be seen playing cricket or football once the heat of the sun eased up. Elderly folk came out for evening strolls. Horses grazed on the grass before being called to duty for pulling carriages, that were rented by couples, looking for romantic sojourns and making memories. The grounds were bordered on one side by immense towers that housed offices and provided the lucky employees working there with a bird's eye view of the wide expansive grounds in front of them, and the river coursing nearly parallel to the grounds a little further away. On another side, tram lines bordered the grounds. Tourists and travelers on this outmoded yet highly romanticized mode of transportation could go around the city at a leisurely pace and see the sights. Well-built roads paved the other borders of the grounds. Due to the freshness and greenery they provided, these grounds had become the lungs of the city.

We walked hand in hand till we crossed the grounds. The whole thing felt organic and there was no awkwardness or hesitation. We were comfortable in silence and enjoyed each other's company, without feeling the urge to be verbose. I knew that I had found someone special.

Soon Sandxira and I saw the local cricket stadium looming in front of us. This was an indication that our destination was mere minutes away. Many a heart had been broken in the stadium when the home team lost matches, and many a cheer had rung through its stands when the home team snatched up victory in the last minute. On game days, these stretches of roads near the stadium were packed with people rushing to fill their seats. Barely enough space was available for a fly to squeeze through. Unwary persons perpetually ran the risk of losing their hearing, on their way to the stadium, in case they accidentally veered too close to anyone who had started ritualistic pre-cheers before the start of the match. The cacophony was often punctuated by the jarring sound of vuvuzelas, that were blown by children aged ten and above; the above included men in their thirties and forties. Cricket was a strange game that drove the viewers mad with blinding passion. As we were walking by, we saw that the place wore a deserted look. A match was not scheduled at the stadium for another couple of months.

A few minutes afterwards, we reached the river bank. The day was quite windy, but not windy enough yet to herald the coming of a storm. The sun had gone down on the opposite bank and twilight was about to set in. Street lamps started to light up at equidistant points on the road. The city architects had favored white LED lights near the river bank, instead of the usual yellow sodium vapor ones that had been installed in the rest of the city. A few meters before reaching the river bank, on the left side of us, there was a Palladian porch. The edifice was supposed to be a memorial dedicated to one of the colonists, who had seemingly played a major role in the development of the city. The man was revered by the native noblemen, who had collectively commissioned the construction of the structure to honor him. The entire edifice was periodically repaired by the authorities. It was a well-known spot in the city where films and music videos were shot. Despite the overt commercialization of the porch, the place did have a unique ineffable charm to it, a charm that was heightened in the slowly approaching dusk.

The river bank itself was one of the most well-maintained places of its kind, in the city. One of the suspension bridges that connected the residential side of the city to the industrial side, loomed over us to the left side of the sky, standing still in an imposing yet dignified manner, like a giant vigilant mothership. The kilometer-long marvel of engineering was starting to light up for travelers in the nearing darkness.

The embankment had large stairs built into it. The stairs went down into the river and disappeared under the water. The lowermost stairs were visible due to low tide being in effect at the moment. These stairs were overgrown with moss and covered with mud. They had skid marks in places where the more adventurous souls had tried to walk, and had slipped, possibly injuring themselves.

We sat down on one of the top steps, next to each other.

"Tell me more about heavy metal music." Sandxira said.

"Are you sure about it? I have a tendency to start monologuing when I talk about it." I cautioned her.

"That I have noticed, but humor me." she replied.

"Well, to me heavy metal music is poetry," I began in earnest, "a lot of heavy metal musicians have been inspired by poets and authors and have adapted the work of such writers into their music. Take for example Iron Maiden's 'Rime of the Ancient Mariner', adapted from the poem of the same name, by Samuel Taylor Coleridge. It is a song about a group of voyagers marooned at sea, who are trying to find the coast. One of the mariners kills an albatross for food, but albatrosses are widely believed by sailors to be good omens and indicate the presence of land nearby. Killing an innocent creature that was trying to help them, brings a barrage of misfortune on the mariners. They turn on their guilty crew member and punish him by making the man wear the dead bird around his neck, so that he may repent and seek forgiveness from the sea, and once the sea is appeased, the mariners would be able to escape its wrath."

She nodded in comprehension.

"Then there is 'Hallowed Be Thy Name', also by Iron Maiden. It is a song about an innocent man who is about to be taken to the gallows and hung till death. He contemplates the life he has led. He has failed to get justice. He wonders why was he not exonerated for a crime he did not commit, and is being led to his doom. When a fellow prisoner wishes that may god be with him, the man wonders, that if there is a god, why is such a god letting an innocent man like him die. There are others like Black Sabbath's 'War Pigs', that speaks of the futility of war, about how the ordinary folk and the foot soldiers become fodders in battles, while the bureaucrats and politicians are hidden away in the comfort of their homes. Metallica's 'One' is about a soldier who has been grievously injured in war, and all he wants is to die. The man has been in a landmine accident. He has lost his sight, his speech, his hearing, his arms and his legs. The man is unable to tolerate the immense pain that he is in and is completely helpless, but he is being forcefully kept alive using artificial means by doctors, out of some misplaced sense of benevolence that they are saving the man." I continued, my eyes blazing, nearly working myself up into a frenzy.

"I really like these high concept songs." Sandxira said.

"My personal favorite among them, and which in a way helped me come to a decision about making changes to my life, has to be 'Paranoid'."

"How come?" she asked.

"The song seems to be like a warning by an old man to his younger self, a bitter man who is filled with regrets. He says that he cannot find satisfaction in anything and is slowly losing his mind. He needs someone to show him the things in life that will give him true happiness and he laments because he thinks that he is blind to such treasures. He cannot feel happiness or love, and ends the song by advising those who are listening to him that they should think of his life as a cautionary tale, and enjoy life while they still can, spend time with their loved ones, follow their passions. He wishes he could do the same but it is too late for him."

"Hmm..." said Sandxira, while looking out at the river.

I shrugged, "Heavy metal music faces a lot of flak from critics, who believe that it is nothing but loud noises and people screaming without any rhyme or reason." I said, "It is actually much more than that. It is a rich tapestry, and the music deals with many mature topics that are usually not dealt with by more mainstream musicians, topics like depression, anxiety, addiction, obsession, infatuation and angst. Many heavy metal musicians are incredibly well educated. Some of them are astrophysicists, some of them are doctors, others are literature professors. Bruce Dickinson of Iron Maiden is even a pilot, and flies the band's very own airplane to concert venues. That guy has literally survived cancer. He is the most metal guy ever."

I made the devil's horn symbol with my index and little finger as I said this. I continued, like I was in a trance and I noticed that Sandxira was looking at me affectionately, waiting to see if I would tire myself out.

"In fact, a professor in an American university uses lyrics of heavy metal songs to teach his students about grammar, because most of the sentence constructions are done immaculately, since a large number of these musicians have been influenced by poets and authors, and are incredibly well read."

Sandxira was silent. "I am so sorry that I have been boring you for the past few minutes." I said apologetically.

"Not at all," she smiled, "I am really glad to be able to listen to you talk about this. It is hard to come by people these days who are so passionate about their interests, and willing to wear such passion on their sleeves." she said to me.

We sat in silence for a while looking out at the river. The darkness was on its way to becoming total as night gradually descended, but there was still adequate light for someone to read a book, were that person so inclined. The buildings on the opposite side of the river were beginning to come to life. The embankment over there was lit up with yellow lamps, as the other side of the river was under the control of a different municipality. The lights from the bridge on our left were reflected in the river below, but the reflection was distorted by the continuous flow of the river, looking like a water color, in which the paint had begun to run. The boats of fishermen and tourists were slowly making their way back to the coast to drop anchor for the night. A hurricane lamp was lit in each of the boats. The lamps barely provided enough light for the oarsmen to be able to see a few feet in front of them. To the people on the river bank, the boats looked like small fireflies floating leisurely on their way back home.

"Do you fancy a walk?" Sandxira asked.

"Sure." I said.

We got back up, dusted our trousers to shake off the dried mud, and started leisurely walking away from the stairs. The path we took was parallel to the river bank, along a cobblestone street.

The street was lined on both sides by small palm trees, barely six feet high. The trees were still in their adolescent stages. Interspersed with the trees were flowering bushes; hibiscuses, sunflowers, ixoras, cherry blossoms, daisies and geraniums. At various points on the side of the pathway, close to the wall across the river bank, steel benches had been set up for visitors to sit on, relax and enjoy a view of the river. At the moment, the benches were populated by couples whispering sweet nothings into each other's ears, and carving their names into the side of the benches. Their aim was to be immortalized and make archaeologists from the future scratch their heads in confusion, when these benches would be dug up from excavation sites, a few thousand years later, to study the ruins of this once great city. Various street side vendors had set up shop and were periodically hawking their fares to bring in customers. The vendors were selling paraphernalia such as toys, roses, balloons, various forms of savories and other cooked food items. Sandxira and I bought an ice cream cone each, I got a chocolate flavored one, and she got a combination of chocolate and vanilla, which I felt that it was kind of a redundant choice as it would deprive each of us, the opportunity to sample what flavor the other had got. She permitted me to pay for the ice creams. For the next few minutes, our attention became focused on the ice cream cones, and we were licking off the sides to prevent runaway streams of ice cream from making our palms sticky.

"What optimistic creatures humans are," Sandxira said contemplatively, "imagine expecting the species to last for millions of years. I sometimes wonder if it is more hubris than optimism, as though people were invariably well designed to last forever," she shrugged, "Well, who knows? What is your guess?" she asked, turning to me.

I had bitten off a chunk of ice cream along with the wafer, "Wha?" I said with my mouth full.

"Do you want to venture a guess about how long the human race will be around?" she asked, licking the bulging ice cream cone.

"Umm... I have never actually given it a serious thought." I said, swallowing the ice cream. I grimaced immediately as I got a momentary brain freeze. Brushing it aside,

I said, "I presume that eventually, the world is going to be run over by giant crabs and insectoids, who will become the dominant species on the planet, maybe by the time one million A.D. rolls around. Or maybe it will be like in the story, the 'Night Lands' where the sun burns itself out, and humanity finds an artificial way to keep the planet warm as they evolve to survive in perpetual darkness, like the Morlocks, only less savage."

"That is an interesting perspective." Sandxira said.

"Why do you ask?"

"Well... I am about to tell you something, that will hopefully help you get some perspective." she said.

"Go on."

"The thing is...I am not of this Universe." she said.

"Come on Come on! Get your pastries while they are warm!" shouted a shopkeeper in the background.

"I see." I said and then unmindfully walked a little ahead. Suddenly the weight of what she had said sunk in, and I stopped in my tracks.

I turned around and looked at Sandxira. Everything behind her seemed to be blurred, like a bokeh portrait. A soft breeze blew her hair in the wind as if in slow motion. I was vaguely aware of the sound of the tiny waves in the flowing river next to us, splashing against the bank, of the sound of hawkers shouting out their fares, and of cars moving on the main road on the other side of the cobblestone street. Despite their varied timbres, all the sounds seemed like an assortment of organized cacophony, that failed to leave any impact on me.

"I am not sure I follow." I said, after processing her revelation for a few minutes.

Sandxira stared at me in silence. A heavier wind had started blowing by then, the skies were darkening with approaching clouds.

"What do you mean you are not of this Universe?" I asked.

She looked at me with her brows slightly creased. An imperceptible smile was playing on her lips.

"You know there are easier ways to tell someone that you would like to be left alone." I said.

"That is not the case at all," Sandxira came forward, took my hand and placed it on her chest. She said, "I have wanted to tell this to you for a very long time. I could not say anything when you had asked me out all those months ago. The fact is I was not sure about you back then, but I have really grown to enjoy your company and I like spending time with you."

I let out a sigh and huffed. A distant part of my brain was unconsciously humming 'Last Night' by Terje Rypdal. It was a piece I had heard a long time ago, while watching the movie 'Heat', but the music had stayed with me. In the movie, this music played over a four-minute sequence where Robert de Niro, after having met Amy Brenneman in a coffee shop, had taken her back to his place on the hills of Los Angeles. The pair were sipping wine and looking out at the city below, which was lit up like a cloudless night sky. The lights seemed to be arranged haphazardly at first glance, but formed constellations of their own, the more the eyes stared at them and the mind began drifting.

"I still do not understand. Why are you telling me this now?" I asked.

"I used to think that what you and I have shared till now was never meant to be. To me, it should not have happened, especially if we take into consideration our differences, yet I find myself increasingly attracted to you and enamored by you. I feel that you deserve to know the truth."

"And what exactly is the truth?" I asked, my voice slightly raised and agitated.

"That I am not of this Universe." Sandxira repeated.

I let the ice cream cone drop from my hand. I raised my hands and interlocked my fingers behind my head. I arched my back, trying to come to terms with what Sandxira had just told me. Then I let my hands fall to my sides. I shook my head, turned away from her and started walking away.

"Just allow me to explain" her voice came from my left. She had caught up to me.

"I don't think there is anything to explain. You can do the decent thing and tell me to my face to leave you alone. You know I will be perfectly happy to do that." I said, picking up my pace.

"I do not want you to leave me alone, I like you and you need to know what I have to say." Sandxira had started walking faster too.

"Whatever it is, I do not think I have it in me to understand what you need to tell me, and I doubt that I will believe it anyway."

Sandxira grabbed my hand and held it. She held it with paranormal strength. I could not budge an inch from where I had been stopped in my tracks. I turned around and looked at Sandxira. I saw that her eyes were blazing. The wind had started to blow faster now, but to me it seemed that her hair had taken up a life of its own, spreading away from her head, like the tentacles of a deep-sea creature. She resembled the wrath of nature in its full fury. Almost as suddenly, her hair fell back down, and of their own will bunched themselves over her right shoulder.

I realized that I was staring at her with my mouth slightly open.

"I am sorry for that, but please, let us go somewhere and talk. I promise you that I will not ask you for anything else after this and you and I can go our separate ways."

"O...Oh kay" I said. I was visibly shaken.

She came forward and hugged me. The pounding in my heart slowed down and I became calmer.

"Okay," I said, "let us talk."

We came to the boat jetty that was some distance ahead of us. Large passenger ferry boats usually docked in the boat jetty. Wooden benches were lined against the side of each ferry boat, and were also arranged in two parallel rows in the center of the boat for the passengers to sit on. The rest of the space on the ferry boats was left empty for the intrepid folk to stand on. Some passengers stored their bicycles in the empty spaces, and various vendors stored their fares. The huge round wicker baskets were stocked with a variety of vegetables, roasted peanuts, savory snacks, and fish.

The river itself gave off a mildly salty and rotten stench that seemed to mask the smell of the fish. All the fares were those that had remained unsold at the end of the day in the market places. The vendors were carrying them back to their homes on the other side of the river, either to sell them off at a cheaper price in another market place, especially for the perishables like fish, or mix them in with freshly prepared fare and bring them back for selling the next day, like the roasted peanuts and assorted savories.

The last boat of the day was leaving from our side of the river to go to the opposite one. We bought our tickets at the counter, and Sandxira bought a bottle of water from an adjacent small shop. We walked over a wooden board that connected the concrete embankment of the boat jetty to the boat, and stepped inside. We found seats for ourselves on the side of the boat and sat down. The boat ride would take half an hour.

While the boat was docked, Sandxira was looking out at the river, her eyes slightly unfocused. It seemed that she was trying to figure out in her head how to explain her situation to me.

When the boat lurched away from the dock, and the dull roar of the motor kicked in, propelling the boat to its destination, she finally turned around and looked at me.

"You know how in your universe, every unit of existence is a collection of even smaller units? The body that you live in, is a collection of cells, a number of bodies living in a geographic area makes a city, a number of cities make a district, and so on till a number of countries make up the planet?"

"Ye..es.." I said, unsure where she was going with this.

"Planets make up a solar system, solar systems make up a galaxy and galaxies make up this universe?"

"I think, I do." I said, beginning to dread where she was headed.

"Well, much like this, even universes are constituents of an even more massive unit. Unfortunately, humans are not equipped with the ability to grasp the concept of the immensity that I am talking about. You tend to believe that everything you know and are aware of, are contained in this universe. There is nothing beyond. Like one giant cosmic balloon that is holding all the galaxies, stars and planets inside, and the outer shape of the balloon is the limits of the universe as perceived or understood by you. Imagine now that what you understand as the universe is not the end, nor is it limitless as some people will have you believe. A number of such balloons comprise, let us say for ease of your understanding, an Ultraverse. I... happen to come from the Ultraverse."

My head reeled. I felt nauseated. I thrust my head over the edge of the boat and hurled. She patted my back as I threw up brownish gastrointestinal fluids. After I was done, I shakily wiped my mouth on a handkerchief, that I was fortunately carrying in my pocket. Sandxira broke the seal of the water bottle and handed it over to me. I took a sip, rinsed my mouth and spat it out, trying to get rid of the acidic taste that lingered in my mouth after the vomit. I rinsed and repeated and then finally took a proper sip and drank a mouthful of water. A few alarmed onlookers had come over trying to see if I was doing okay. I weakly assured everyone that I had recovered from my bout of nausea, and the people dispersed.

"How are you feeling?" Sandxira asked.

"Not great," I confessed, "I am having major difficulty trying to come to terms with the idea of the Ultraverse."

"Good" she said and smiled at me, "because I was messing with you."

I looked at her with a stupefied expression on my face. This girl, or whatever she actually was, was starting to get on my nerves. I briefly had a mental image in my head of me hoisting her up by her waist and throwing her into the river.

"Why must you do this to me?" I asked weakly.

"I am not from an Ultraverse. In fact, I do not even know how reliable that explanation of the Ultraverse is that I just gave to you. But the fact is I am not of this Universe. I am from a place that is somewhere adjacent to this Universe, an alternate dimension if you will."

"If you say so" I said, with a hopeless tone. Things had stopped making any sense a while ago and I could only go with the flow.

"I want you to have all the facts, and not be under any misconception that I am trying to blow you off or trying to manipulate you into leaving me alone. I would hate for you to think that." Sandxira said.

"Fair enough."

The darkening sky and increased wind speed began to rock the boat slightly. The waves of the river began splashing against the boat and sent up mists of water that sprayed the passengers inside. We held on to the wooden railing on the side of the boat.

"I am, what you may understand as, a disembodied consciousness, "said Sandxira, "not a ghost or a spirit, as some believers on this planet understand it, but an entity who has evolved beyond the need for a physical body, unlike an entity like you, who needs a physical body to exist.

"The fact is, I do not know when our universe began, or whether it would even come to an end. We have tried to understand its nature, but when beings of our race came into existence, our universe itself had become so ancient that any background radiations that would have helped us understand or know when the universe began, had long dissipated. So, we gave up trying to understand the nature of our universe, and began our research into the multiverse. Are you familiar with the concept of the multiverse?" she asked me.

"Only from what I have read in graphic novels, science fiction books or seen in movies." I replied.

"And that is?" Sandxira asked.

"That there exists, multiple universes, one on top of each other, like giant pancakes laid out in a stack on a plate. There are two main theories of how multiverses work. One theorizes that each individual universe is completely different and dissociated from another, having its own creation myth, its own set of physical laws, its own set of celestial bodies, and its own separate indigenous life forms. The other theorizes that the multiverse is a result of the choices of an individual, that the universe branches out into new paths, every time an individual, when faced with choices, exercises one choice over the others. Therefore, the prime universe is the result of an individual making pre-determined choices, and the multiverse is the result of exercise of alternate choices by the individual. Infinite choices, infinite universes." I exposited.

Sandxira looked at me with glowing admiration on her face. "I can see why I like you." she said.

In spite of everything, I felt myself blushing at the compliment.

"However, the fact is," she continued, "a choice based multiverse is a fallacy, because for a person to become aware of such a multiverse, he would have to meet some version of himself from an alternate reality. Let's call this person X. This means that every choice that members of a race such as humanity has made in the alternate reality, or even the supposedly inanimate objects in such reality itself, has been pre-determined up to that point to result in the conception of the person X, and to facilitate a circumstance through which he would become aware of, or come in contact with his own self, but from the prime universe. Do you follow me so far?" Sandxira asked.

Despite the surreal nature of the situation that I had found myself in, Sandxira's explanation seemed surprisingly lucid. I nodded to show understanding.

"So it must follow that if billions of years of existence and pre-determined incidents has led to a situation where two selves of an individual meet and become aware of the multiverse, it is unlikely that events would, going forward in the alternate reality, be any different from the prime universe considering that everything that had happened till then in the alternate reality has been pre-determined, and it is the nature of the prime universe itself to proceed in a pre-determined manner? Any change that might occur in the trajectory of a given universe as a result of an event so insignificant as the meeting of the two selves from parallel universes, would be the equivalent of a river's course completely changing its direction because a grain of rice was dropped into it. Are we good till now?"

"Yes", I said, comprehension dawning.

"So, it follows that the alternate reality itself has also been functioning in a pre-determined manner, and will continue to function in such a pre-determined manner, absolutely identical in nature to the prime universe. Therefore, a choice based multiverse, as you may theorize, is a non-starter paradox, because every universe in such a model functions absolutely identical to each other."

"If I understand it correctly, what you are saying is that there is no free will in the universe, and we all function in a set pre-determined manner?"

"No. I am saying that every entity in a universe, whether it is my universe or your universe, that has consciousness, exerts free will of its own, and every incident that has ever happened till date or will ever happen in the future is absolutely different from the one preceding it. The multiverse exists, but each universe is entirely different from the other."

"And you are a disembodied consciousness from one such parallel universe." I repeated.

"Yes, I am." Sandxira affirmed, "So, as I was telling you, we soon realized that trying to understand the origin of our universe was a non-starter. Our universe is a dark one that is devoid of light of any kind. When our race came into existence, all the luminous bodies in our universe had already burnt themselves up and had become cold dead masses or massive singularities that devoured everything around them. The best way to understand such bodies is to picture immense black circles that appear to rotate upon themselves at incredibly high speeds, looming up at distant points in the sky, where your own twinkling stars are visible. The singularities themselves are not visible by our perception of sight, but by the roaring piercing sounds they make during their incredibly high speed rotations, sucking up various debris around it and the piercing winds that result from it. On certain occasions, we often shudder at the sound of such howling stars, when they pass close to us, close in astronomical terms that is."

"Are you talking about black holes?" I asked.

"That would be the closest approximation of such celestial bodies in your Universe, yes." Sandxira replied.

"Wait. How do such stars make roaring piercing sounds? Isn't space supposed to be vacuum? How is there any sound at all?" I asked.

"Space as it exists in my universe, is not empty vacuum as it is here. The space in my universe consists of what you feel and comprehend as air. It has the same property of heating up on application of pressure or cooling down upon release of pressure, and the tendency of blowing from a place of high pressure, to a place of low pressure resulting in what you understand as winds. Our race has learnt the way of harnessing the power of such strong currents, and that helps us to travel in the interstellar medium. Interstellar of course is a misnomer considering the absence of stars, but you understand what I am trying to say."

"To an extent yes." I nodded, "You guys are like mariners of the heavens in your universe."

"That is fairly accurate. Ours is a dark dilapidated universe that continues to expand like a ripple on the surface of an immense black cosmic lake."

She let the words sink in. I was looking at her, and she was looking out towards the river. Something about the way she told me everything, made me feel that that she was being truthful about it all. Here I was, an ordinary man, having done absolutely ordinary things in life, having never tried to seek answers to the mysteries of the universe, except occasionally immersing myself in works of fiction. Here I was in the presence of, for lack of a better word, entity, who was not only the answer to the question, "Are we alone", but also to the question, "Is our universe everything there is". And, I had no idea why she was telling me all this.

Our boat had approached the underside of another bridge over the river, that ran nearly parallel to the previous bridge, in the shadow of which we had sat down and talked about heavy metal music, a couple of hours ago. Life was so uncomplicated back then.

This bridge was another marvel of architecture as well, one of the longest on the planet. It had been built by riveting the entire structure, without installing any nuts or bolts anywhere. This bridge was one of the landmarks of the city, and like the Palladian porch from before, this bridge too was regularly featured in movies and videos that were shot in the city. Its absence made such works of art feel incomplete, at least to the makers. As we passed close to the belly of the beast, the bridge loomed up with an intimidating gothic presence, having a much more visceral design than the bridge from before, like a massive steel sentinel. Sandxira's face occasionally lit up with the bright light of the sodium vapor lamps that lined the sidewalks of the bridge. The last time I had seen this happen, had been when she and I were discussing about pedestrian matters, such as stressful jobs.

We crossed the bridge soon. The lights of the boat jetty on the opposite river bank had become visible in the distance. Faint sounds of the busy people on the boat jetty were coming across the river to us.

She finally turned back towards me, smiled again and resumed.

"So, we began our research into the existence of the multiverse. Surely, we figured, there would be other universes with properties similar or identical to ours, that were still in their nascent stages of development or were just of the right age so that such universes could help us understand and make conclusions about the nature of our own universe.

"We realized that our universe has a fundamental wave pattern, or vibration, a vibration that permeates the very fabric of the space time that constitutes our realm. If there was a way that we could harness this fundamental wave pattern, and cause an object in our universe to resonate with another wave pattern that was the fundamental vibration of a universe adjacent to ours, theoretically when the vibration of the object fell out of resonance and took up the fundamental wave pattern of the adjacent universe, the object could travel to the alternate universe from ours. This is what we called phasing.

"Our researchers worked tirelessly and finally succeeded in their experiments, through which they transferred a minuscule object from our universe to another. Serendipitously, that universe was your universe. However, that event was an uncontrolled phasing. There was empty vacuum in the corresponding place in your universe where the object phased in. We were unable to control and lower the energy of the vibrating object. The vibrations inadvertently converted to kinetic energy and the object got hurled through space at an immense speed, without any resistance to slow it down. The object crashed on this planet of yours and caused a world ending event. This event is recorded in your history as the asteroid strike that destroyed the dinosaurs."

I was hooked on the narration by now.

"After that cataclysmic event, we became so ashamed of our actions, that research into the existence of the multiverse was put on hold indefinitely."

At this point, it appeared that her voice cracked a little. Probably the shame of having accidentally caused a genocide had resurfaced in her mind as a painful race memory. I reached out, and held her hand, giving it a little squeeze.

"Of course, our researchers did not know of the mass extinction event back then. It was kind of like a kid hitting a ball for a six out of the park, and then running away and hiding himself because he is sure that the rogue ball will end up breaking someone's window, and he does not want to be caught and blamed for it. Even though research into the multiverse had been indefinitely put on hold, evolution continued at its own pace. Our race soon evolved into disembodied consciousnesses. But we are not a hive mind. Every entity has its own separate consciousness. Having shed the need for a physical body, we thought that it would make it easier to phase between universes. We were wrong again. The first few travelers who tried to phase into different universes were immediately torn apart and destroyed by the physical laws of the universe that they were visiting. We realized that to be able to travel between universes, we would need to take the form of an entity that was a native resident of the universe which we were visiting, at the particular point in time and space, like needing to take the form of human beings if we were visiting this planet."

"So, if you visited 500 million years ago, you would have to take the form of sea creatures?" I could not contain my curiosity.

"That is roughly accurate, even though we did not have the necessary technology so long ago." Sandxira said. "Once we had worked out the kinks and began full-fledged inter-dimensional travel, we searched far and wide for a universe that resembled ours, and had identical or similar physical laws. We persisted for a long time, but every universe we visited was as completely alien and different to ours as our universe would be to yours. It was then that we were reminded of the deterministic nature of our own universe, that our universe was completely unique and every event that had happened prior to the coming into existence of our race had happened to bring our universe to the state that it was in. The fundamental vibration of our universe was unique to itself, and would not be found anywhere else, which made our pursuit of seeking out a universe that was similar to ours, futile and inconsequential. There was no other universe similar to ours in existence. Probably on a subconscious level, we were aware of this, otherwise our researchers would have never considered the idea of relying on the fundamental vibrations of universes as the method of inter-dimensional travel in the first place."

"What did you do then?" I asked intrigued. I realized that I had never listened to her speak continuously like this ever. I had always done the major share of the talking while she listened to me.

"After the acceptable period of mourning that a race is allowed, when it realizes that it has been barking up a tree that never existed in the first place, we resigned ourselves to the fact that it was futile to try and attempt to understand the nature of our universe. We were extremely far ahead in the future of our realm. Hence, we decided to be chroniclers of the multiverse. Now, we visit various parts of the multiverse, observe the indigenous conscious beings that reside therein, enmesh ourselves in their civilizations and make notes of the prevalent physical laws and general composition of that universe. We keep detailed records of the same."

"Why? What would be the point of that?" I asked.

"I like to believe that this approach was adopted as an act of altruism that we felt we owed the denizens of the multiverse. A form of penance if you will, for meddling with the nature of space time of various universes, and causing the inadvertent extinction of the dinosaurs. As far as we know, no other life forms in the multiverse has developed inter-dimensional travel. When they do, and if they come across our universe, it will make their understanding of the multiverse a lot easier and make them aware of any hurdles or dangers that they might find in their travels. For instance, did you know that there is a universe that can fit in the entirety of this droplet of water on my palm?" Sandxira said, holding up her palm to my face, nestled on which was a droplet of water that had accumulated from the mists that the boat had sprayed up from the river, "or that there is a universe which is comprised entirely of fire, that burns endlessly and perpetually, reaching entropic death in a matter of a thousand years as opposed to trillions of years?"

"Woah" I said, in an unintentional imitation of a well-known movie star.

"So yes, we became observers of the multiverse, and it was my assignment to visit your planet and study it for the purpose of our records. I have been here for quite some time now."

"Considering that the universes are constantly evolving, at least ours is, you would need to come back to the same place from time to time, I reckon, to record the changes? Like coming up with new updated editions of previous books, or like in our legal field, coming up amendments or overhauls to the existing laws in place?" I asked.

"Yes, we do. It is an ongoing process that we are engaged in and it will go on for eons. I may be required to come back to this Universe a few thousand years in the future, long after everything we see around us right now are gone and have become dust. Honestly, I really like this Universe because it is so young, vibrant, bright and warm. Even the stars are barely out of their adolescence. Makes me hopeful."

This made me feel slightly sad. In a way I was coming to terms with my own mortality and realizing how truly insignificant I was in the scheme of all of existence. It really made my personal trials and tribulations seem myopic, pointless and selfish.

By now we had come within docking distance of the boat jetty on the other side of the river. The boat helper skillfully jumped from the starboard side of the boat onto the concrete embankment, carrying a thick heavy length of jute rope. He landed a little more heavily than he had intended to, his rubber slippers making a sharp crack- ing sound against the concrete, and in a swift motion, he proceeded to tie the rope around a broad column, while the boat driver gently steered and parked the boat into the jetty. We got up from our seats and followed a group of women carrying vegetables on wicker baskets on their heads, out of the boat and onto mainland.

We walked ensconced in the thick crowd, being driven forward by the current of the people, rather than making any conscious effort to chart our own way. After a hundred meters, the crowd thinned, and we could finally break away. We began walking towards the taxi stand and after a short while Sandxira put a hand on my shoulder.

"Would you mind taking the bus?" she asked, "we would be much less conspicuous."

I agreed. We changed directions and began walking towards the bus stand.

The clouds that had gathered a while ago, indicating a potential thunderstorm, had been emblematic of a false alarm and had dissipated. The sky had cleared up and two or three stars were visible through the dense pollution.

"Can I ask you something? I hope you will not find it offensive or insensitive." I said cautiously.

"Of course," she said.

"I am sorry if this appears tactless and immature after everything you have told me, but are you an entity of what we, at least on this planet, perceive as the female gender?"

She looked at me, blinked a few times, and then burst out laughing.

"Well, I *am* an entity from another universe." she said, "We have evolved beyond the concepts of gender identity, but we tend to adapt to the gender limitations of the universe that we are inhabiting at a particular place and time. You would not believe how many genders exist in your own universe among other civilizations, let alone in other parts of the multiverse."

"Fair enough. I do not know why I asked that. I feel attracted to you nevertheless." I confessed.

She hugged me around my midriff and pecked me on my cheek.

We found a relatively empty bus. Fortunately, the bus would take us through a route that would be common for both Sandxira and I. She could get down at her stop and I could continue on to mine.

"Would you like to be taken on a tour of the multiverse sometime?" she asked half-jokingly.

I looked at her and shrugged with a smile. "It is strangely poetic," I observed, "that description of your universe, of being in a state of continuous expansion across the surface of an immense black cosmic lake. Somehow haunting and melancholic. There is a strange inescapable inevitability to it, a loneliness. Maybe that will be our fate, when this universe reaches entropic death. This planet here will eventually become a dark frozen graveyard, orbiting a cinder."

Sandxira's hand reached out and held my hand. Her fingers interlocked with mine. She laid her head on my left shoulder. Neither of us wanted to say anything to each other. We just wanted to stay immersed in the silence of each other's company, and stare out at the river as the bus crossed the steel sentinel bridge and entered the city, picking up and dropping off passengers on its route. The conductor of the bus stood at the door, shouting out the stops that the bus would be passing through in an attempt to bring in passengers. He kept running his thumb over the top of the bundle of tickets that he held in his hand. It made the sound of paper being flipped through at really high speeds. I used to love that sound as a kid. The onomatopoeic representation of that sound in my head was '*frrrk frrrk*'.

When Sandxira's destination came close, she turned and looked expectantly at me. Both of us got up from our seats and headed to the door of the bus, stopping at the door to pay for our tickets. We got down from the bus when Sandxira's stop arrived.

We walked towards her apartment hand in hand.

PART 8: A BREEZE IN THE NIGHT

Sandxira and I took the elevator up to the flat that she was renting. Her apartment was on the fourth floor of the building. The place was sparsely furnished. The kitchen was on the left, just as we entered through the front door. It had been fitted with state-of-the-art modular kitchen facilities. There were shelves that slid out, on which grooves had been carved in for storing utensils. The hall was quite big and doubled up as a drawing room as well as a dining room, depending on how the furniture was arranged. Next to the wall opposite the balcony, was a rectangular dining table with four chairs. Perpendicular to the dining table was a refrigerator of medium size. A sofa and bean bag covered up some additional space in the gargantuan hall. There was no television in the room. Who needs something so pedestrian when one has travelled and seen things in the multiverse, things which are beyond the scope of imagination of mere humans?

She led me by the hand to her bedroom. It was dark inside, but we did not feel the need to switch on the lights. Gradually our eyes got accustomed to the darkness. Sandxira lightly kissed me, as if to tease. She proceeded to undress and got into bed with her knees tucked up in front of her. I undressed and joined her. She lay on the bed, arms reaching out to hold me, her back arched, submitting herself to my embrace. She had a very distinct sweet smell that I found very familiar but could not identify at that moment. I was feeling a little self-conscious, not being in peak physical shape. Even though I had started an exercise regimen, it was taking some time to show results. My man breasts, that were eighty per cent on their way to becoming pectoral muscles, were swinging slightly in a haphazard and embarrassing motion as I moved my body over hers. Her body seemed to stiffen with ecstasy as a soft moan escaped her lips. I reached up and kissed her neck and her nails dug into my back as she pulled me in and held me tightly to her. I could feel my own distended belly pressed against her nearly flat one and made a mental note to double down on the exercise regimen.

I was eager to please Sandxira and her pleasure became my only goal as I worked tirelessly. We were surprisingly working well together, moving fluidly, each of us seeming to sense what the other was about to do. It seemed that we had found our rhythm. When I moved too quickly and bumped my nose on her chin, we laughed quietly, rubbing the spots.

Later when I went in search for a cold liquid from the fridge, she came too. She opened the freezer, popped an ice cube into her mouth and kissed me. The cold lips proceeded to caress my neck, then my chest and came back once again to my lips.

Back in bed we kissed some more and then began all over again. The air between us had lost its nervous charge and we were able to enjoy ourselves. If I had a music system at hand, I would have been playing 'Just Like Roses' by the Cruzados as we became intimate. Sandxira moved on top, straddling me, her legs around my hips. She was facing me and slowly increasing her rhythm, until all I could do was lie back with my eyes closed, holding on tightly to the bedsheets. Her breath escaped with a hiss. As we reached completion, she arched her back and neck, while her hands were pressed down upon my chest. Still entangled, I rose up from the bed, embraced her, and kissed her neck at every place that I could reach. Soon we were pawing at each other's faces like inexperienced teenagers lost in euphoria.

I laid down on the bed, my right arm spread out. Sandxira laid down beside me, her head on my arm and her right hand on my chest. Her mane of curly hair covered the right side of my face. She ran her hand over my chest, twirling the long hairs with her index finger. She reached out and kissed me on my cheek. I turned towards her and kissed her deeply. When we broke, I caressed her cheek with my left hand and she rubbed against it.

"Till date, probably the happiest, unfiltered and uncomplicated memory of my life was the time when my high school crush had confessed to me that she liked me back. We were in the seventh standard back then," I said, "but that memory has a serious competition now."

Sandxira playfully bit my ear and grinned.

"I have some tough competition to beat." she said.

"This is way better than my glacial approach." I said.

"What is that?"

"Oh, it is nothing. A joke really that I had made once with Xeala. She had asked me how I was planning to approach you, and I said that I plan to do so when the glaciers melt, the seas rise, drown everything, cause a mass extinction event, and only then was I going to have the courage to approach you."

"I am glad that both of us changed our minds." Sandxira said.

We lay quietly in each other's arms for some time, savoring the moments.

"Can I ask you something about the multiverse?" I asked.

"Yes?"

"Is it possible that all these works of fiction that we humans have on this planet, which depict their own fictional universes, could these actually exist in the multiverse, if the number of universes in the multiverse is theoretically infinite?"

"Well, we do not know for sure if the multiverse is truly infinite, we are still working out the science," Sandxira said, "but yes, theoretically, it is possible that every fictional universe has found form in some manner in the multiverse. One of my acquaintances discovered a universe where the planets were flat discs which rested on the backs of four elephants, which in turn stood on the back of a gigantic cosmic turtle that swam through space."

I looked at her with a stupefied expression on my face.

"I am joking," she laughed, her eyes twinkling, "it is so easy to mess with you now that the truth is out."

I started tickling her. I tickled her so hard that she doubled up with laughter and pushed my hand away.

"So how did you find yourself here in this place in space time and working as lawyer in a law firm?" I asked.

"I have to keep it interesting or existence, even in the endless possibilities of the multiverse, can get boring." Sandxira said. "This time I wanted to figure out what it would be like to work as a lawyer in the corporate law practice, so I joined our former workplace to experience the work and life there, in order to chronicle it. Turns out that it is not all that it is made out to be. It would certainly not be among my top recommendations for a job that I would make to any associate of mine who might want to come to this planet and try blending in. Besides, the work did not really pose a challenge for me."

"I am guessing nothing would be a challenge for someone who can bend the rules of space and time." I said.

Sandxira shrugged and said, "So, after I got bored in the year that I was there, I decided to move out and work as an in-house corporate counsel to see how different it was."

"Based on what you have told me till now and your decision to quit, I am guessing that it has not been as fulfilling either."

"That it has not been, but I have gathered enough material for my chronicles, and have developed an in depth understanding of how corporate lawyers work."

"But how do you know that this office and their in-house corporate counsel culture it's all there is, and it is similar for every place else?" I asked.

"I only need a sample space understanding for my chronicles. In the grand scheme of things, this is like studying the behavior of an ant. You observe how one ant behaves in reaction to external stimuli such as hunger, pain, temptation or joy and based on your observations you form theories on how ants may act in general. You don't go around observing every individual ant and try to draw distinctions and comparisons between the behaviors of separate ants. It is cumbersome, unnecessary and a waste of resources."

"Oh... I see." I said.

"In fact," she said, with a slight hesitation, "the reason that I am quitting my job is because I have been given another assignment, and it is not in your universe.

"Oh..."

Sandxira took my hand, interlocking her fingers with mine, held them to her lips and kissed the back of my hand.

"But now I am thinking things over" she said and smiled her enticing, ravishing, nubile yet innocent smile, "now that this is turning out to be my favorite assignments till now."

I leaned forward and kissed her. Then I kept planting small kisses till I reached her breasts. Her hands had turned hungry, grasping and digging softly with her nails at my flanks now. Our bodies rubbed against each other. Her hand had reached up to the back of my head and had grabbed a clump of hair in her grasp. I kissed her deeply, my hands exploring her body in all the places that they could reach, while I kept rhythm. When I reached completion, there was an explosive euphoria, that seemed to have more to do with the person shuddering under me than could be attributed to my body's own physiological reaction.

We lay next to each other. The night wind had blown aside the curtain over the open windows, and the street light from outside cast a yellowish glow on Sandxira's face. I reached out and ran my finger through her hair, massaging my fingers deep into her scalp. She seemed to be enjoying it and moaned appreciatively. To her it was like an ecstasy chaser after the climax of lovemaking. She turned away from me, grabbed my wrist and draped my hand over her breasts. Her head was on my arm. She pressed her back against my bare chest. I deeply inhaled her hair and stared out of the window. It had begun to drizzle slightly, and tiny droplets of rain passed through the beam of light cast by the sodium vapor lamp on the street outside. Soon I was fast asleep.

~

Sandxira insisted on making me breakfast in the morning, despite my polite insistence that I could arrange breakfast for myself from somewhere else. She made eggs and toast. I had never really mastered the art of frying the perfect egg and usually ended every dismal effort by dismantling the awkwardly shaped egg with the broken yolk, into smaller potions and passed the dish off as scrambled eggs. Sandxira, on the other hand, did an expert job on the eggs, cooking up perfectly round bull's eye eggs, like she was an expert short order cook, which I figured that she may have been at some point of time, chronicling the profession for her records.

She was wearing a blue kimono that came down to her knees. She had put it on in front of me in the morning, and I knew that she was wearing nothing underneath. Her hair was tied up in a knot over her head and held in place by a single hair pin. I was leaning on the door frame of the kitchen in my shorts and the t-shirt from the previous night, my eyes following her as she went around cracking the eggs on the hot grill and putting the bread pieces in the toaster. Her sight drove me mad with passion, till my reverie was interrupted by the enticing smell of food.

As I sat down to it, Sandxira regarded me with her eyes from across the dining table. I was hungry and ate quickly. Somehow all the pretenses of poise and delicacy seemed to have gone away.

"Did you like it last night?" She asked.

I waited to reply to her, till I could safely gulp down the big mouthful of food without choking on it.

"Yes, I did very much." I blurted out like an excited school boy, before realizing what I had done and blushed slightly.

She threw her head back and laughed, her white teeth glistening in the morning sun. She reached out, cupped my face in her hands and kissed me. She left her chair and came and sat on my lap. My hand moved over her back feeling every inch of it covered by a thin film of cloth. She turned and looked at me.

"What are your plans for the day?" Sandxira asked.

"Nothing," I said with a non-committal shrug, "nothing at all.".

"Good. Are you done with breakfast?" She asked.

Then without waiting for me to answer, she cleared away the plate, took my hand and led me back to her bedroom.

I was sore when I left, feeling like I had just trained for a marathon. As I went down the first flight of stairs, I turned around and waved at her. She waved back at me and blew a kiss.

PART 9: A CRASH COURSE IN FRINGE SCIENCE

"Can you take me with you sometime when you phase?" I asked.

We were lying down on my bed and looking at a ray of light that was coming in from my bedroom window. The ray of light split into smaller beams as it passed through our interlocked fingers, that formed a tepee.

"You still think I am messing with you after all this?" Sandxira asked with a mischievous expression on her face.

"To be fair, I have not seen anything 'extraordinary' to convince me otherwise," I said, using my free hand to make an air quote, raising the stakes.

Sandxira used her free hand to punch me playfully.

"Cards on the table, it does not matter to me where you are from, or who you are. You are here right now with me, for me. That is all I care about." I said earnestly.

She looked at me endearingly.

"I am curious though. Why me? Why have you told me all this? What made you decide that I should know all these intimate details about you? Why did you not let me be a footnote in your existence?" I asked.

Sandxira caressed my face with the back of her hand.

"There is an odd sincerity about you." she said. "You are good with those you care for, and you respect and give people their space. You are passionate about the things you enjoy and are willing to inform and teach others who know less than you, without being condescending to them for their lack of knowledge or being precious about yours. You are clear about what you want, even if it means needing to make compromises for it, like making major career decisions. But you are not fickle minded and you make decisions after careful consideration. These are qualities in you that I found to be very enticing, admirable and attractive. You are not sore on the eyes either." Sandxira said, winking at me.

"Thank you?" I said, a little uncertainly with mild surprise. It seemed that those close to me were more perceptive of my qualities, than I was about them myself.

"A lot of people that I have met over the years try to change to fit into the situation they are in." she continued. "Such change is not always organic, and has been more as a result of survival instincts. Take for instance a junior laughing sycophantically at his boss's inappropriate joke just to be in his good books, or mistreating someone lower than him in the office food chain because of a misplaced sense of superiority and a misguided attempt at trying to establish dominance. While adaptation is definitely an admirable trait, you lose the essence of the person you are and become someone completely different. It is like you are hiding yourself to suit someone else's vision of you.

"There are others that I have met who find it difficult to segregate relationships and usually mess them up by either making advances towards a friend of the opposite gender or actively sabotaging the friendship when their advances are not reciprocated.

"Somehow you have avoided all these landmines and have come out on the other side as quite an attractive person. I did not want whatever we have right now to begin with a deception or be based on one. If you would have chosen to walk away from me after getting to know all this, I would have been fine with it, but I wanted you to make an informed decision." Sandxira said.

"I understand." I said.

We lay in silence for some time.

"Come on," she said, "Let me show you something."

"What is it?"

"Get up and lie back on the bed. I will show you how I phase in and out of universes."

I excitedly got up and did as instructed. I was like a kid who had been promised a magic show on his birthday.

She slid out of the bed sheet and stood up on her feet, shielding the light with her naked body. She walked away from my bed and sat on a chair that was adjacent to my study table.

"Are you watching closely?" she asked.

In front of my eyes, her outline started to become blurry. At first it was negligible. Slowly the vibrations started increasing. Soon her physical form appeared to be fractured, one form overlapping with the other. It was like looking at a television screen that was displaying picture through a broken cathode ray tube and was causing a parallax error. In a few moments, the two forms started vibrating more violently, till they seemed to completely overlap and become one. For a fraction of a second, Sandxira's form stood still. Then she disappeared in the blink of an eye.

I was staring at the spot where she had disappeared with my mouth hanging open. It took me a few moments to realize that Sandxira's phasing had blown the sheets off my bed, knocked over a table lamp and dislodged a stack of loose papers from my table. It looked like a minor hurricane had passed through the room.

A minute later, the fallen lamp on the ground started shaking, papers started flying and with a minor "*zhup*" Sandxira phased back into my room. In her hand, she held an object that looked like a purple polyhedron. She beckoned me to approach her. "It is perfectly safe, you can come over." she said.

I slowly approached her, and she placed the object in my hand. It had a soft velvet like touch.

"This is an object that we consume, from my universe," She said, "the equivalent of this in your universe would be a fruit. It gives us sustenance. Of course, I brought this in without any proper phasing clearance, so it attained an approximation of a form that it would ideally have, if it existed in the natural order of this universe."

"This is fantastic," I said as I looked at the fruit in my palm, awed and excited.

"Without proper phasing clearance, this object will not be able to sustain itself in this universe. Watch." she said.

Looking at my hand, I saw that the object was starting to turn red.

"Ah!" I exclaimed and dropped the fruit in panic. In front of my eyes, the fruit gradually started turning into floating red wisps, that rose into the air and slowly disappeared.

"WOAH!" I said again, in yet another unintentional imitation of the well-known movie star.

"Let me get you something bigger," she said, and phased out again.

This time I could feel my room shaking, when she tried to phase back in.

However, when the "*zhup*" sounded, and Sandxira came back into view, her two forms still appeared to be fractured. She seemed to be in pain. She buckled down the moment she came back, on top of the chair, as if she was in agony. As I came closer to help her, she held out one hand, telling me to stay back. After a few tense seconds, her two forms stabilized and aligned into one. She looked up, winded and exhausted, like she had gone through some terrible ordeal. I kneeled in front of her and put a hand on her shoulder. She immediately drew back. I drew back reflexively as well, worried that I may have done something wrong. Her breath slowly became normal, and she leaned over and hugged me. She hugged me tightly as if she had just escaped mortal danger.

Her hands had been empty when she phased back in.

~

"Are you feeling better?" I asked. I had put a shawl around Sandxira, then stepped out and brought her back a glass of water. She took a nervous sip.

"Ye..es" she said.

I perched myself on the window sill of my bedroom, while she continued to take small sips from the glass. She finally finished, looked up at me, and smiled tremulously.

I pulled up a chair, sat next to her and put my arm around her.

"What happened?" I asked softly.

"I don't know. This has never happened before. We have worked tirelessly to make the phasing happen as seamlessly as possible, and this kind of fracturing has not happened in ages." Sandxira said, shaking her head.

"Any idea what may have caused it?"

"I will have to get someone to run checks, but I am scared to phase back now. I will have to wait for a few days."

"Okay." I said softly, and proceeded to rub her shoulder.

The next few days, we passed in talking to each other. We did not undertake any strenuous physical exertions, as we were not sure what had caused the phasing issue. Meanwhile Sandxira regaled me with stories of her travels to other universes, some of them too outlandish and bizarre to be put into words, some of them oddly familiar, such as her tale of a universe of complete chaos, that drove anyone passing through it completely mad. A few of the early explorers of her universe had come back from the chaos realm, having been terribly corrupted. The explorers intended to corrupt Sandxira and others as well, but were destroyed into nothingness with promptness and extreme prejudice. She told me the tale of another universe that resembled representations of heaven, as depicted in scriptures and discussed in world religions. It brought up the question, whether any being from that universe had inadvertently or purposefully arrived into ours at some point in the distant past and began to be worshipped as gods. Maybe Sandxira and her kin were not the only ones adept at interdimensional travel. The other question was where did the soul actually go after leaving our bodies in this universe. Did the souls move to another entirely different plane of existence, or did they merely phase into another adjacent universe? There were also universes that Sandxira told me about which could fit inside the full stop at the end of this sentence. Such universes were still teeming with life and had their own set of physical laws. The discussions with Sandxira were really invigorating, and made me question the very nature of reality and existence.

I was trying to keep her mind off the phasing incident. It had been a strange and stressful experience for her and was something that she would probably need to take care of, but I secretly wanted her to defer it for the time being. I was selfishly afraid that the next time she phased out of our universe, she might not be able to phase back in.

I suggested to her that we could catch a movie. She agreed to it quite enthusiastically. Probably she did not mind me trying to keep her occupied as well. When browsing for options, I had rather tactlessly and unthinkingly suggested a movie about dinosaurs, but I was slightly taken aback when she agreed to my suggestion.

"Are you sure?" I asked her, "I thought it would be difficult for you to watch the movie. I forgot about the whole incident of your people accidentally killing off the dinosaurs while trying to discover inter-dimensional travel. It would be kind of like asking a descendant of a Nazi to watch a movie about resurrected survivors of the Holocaust." I said.

"That is sweet of you for being so considerate, and that was an oddly demented comparison I may add, but it is a work of fiction that has no basis in reality." she said.

We were playing quite fast and loose with the word "reality" I thought to myself.

"Besides, dinosaurs may not even have looked like the creatures as shown in the movie. The estimation of your scientists about how dinosaurs looked, has been from the study of fossils, from an analysis of the climatic and geographic conditions of prehistoric times, as well as from information about how dinosaurs would have had to adapt themselves in terms of diet and physiology to survive in those conditions. For all intents and purposes, they could have been covered with feathers instead of having the scaly reptilian representation as popular culture depicts them to have," Sandxira said, "it would be like forming a fictionalized image of humans in your head, that they were born with octopus tendrils, wings made of cartilage and talons in place of nails."

"Fair enough." I said.

She picked the movie theatre and the evening time of the show. The theatre was located in a shopping mall which was the only one in the city with her favorite dessert place. The movie was to be followed with a trip for cinnamon rolls. I have never personally understood the appeal of cinnamon; I find the taste of it offensive. It probably has something to do with me having had travel sickness as a ten-year-old kid on a long distance bus journey and vomiting violently on the way. After my first episode, my mother had offered a piece of gum to me which she had thought was mint flavored. The packaging on the gum was quite misleading, being one of those cheap colorful varieties of imported chewing gums that are available at bus stands and train stations. Unfortunately for me, it had a very strong cinnamon flavor. Regurgitated stomach acid and cinnamon is a conflicting and horrifying combination. The gum exacerbated my travel sickness and made the ten hours long travel a hellish experience. Since then I have been wary of cinnamon in any of my food. For me, cinnamon is like a cricket player; I understand the appeal and I will not take it away from anyone, yet I will never stand in line to get cinnamon's autograph. However, Sandxira was the only one for whom I was willing to make an exception and bite the bullet.

The movie itself was quite unremarkable. For a tentpole action movie for which the studio had given carte blanche on the budget, the story, action beats and acting was quite forgettable and at times cringeworthy. In fairness to the makers, there were a few remarkable sequences, like an exploding volcano on the island and lava rushing down the side of the volcano, as the prehistoric creatures jumped over a cliff into the ocean below to escape a fiery demise. I was even mildly invested when the chiseled hero dodged stampeding diplodocus and spinosauruses, rescued his lady love and joined the lemur like parade of dinosaurs by jumping from a large cliff onto the water below. I was even surprised to feel a slight lump in my throat when a brontosaurus was silhouetted in a cloud of ash, following the volcanic carnage, before it let out a mournful call and was engulfed in flames. But the movie lost me soon after. The plot took a very strange left turn in the second half and became a haunted house horror movie with dinosaurs. It must have been an interesting concept on paper, but the execution was uneven and there was no eventual pay off.

Despite the shortcomings of the movie, I could not have wished for better company. There is something strangely sweet and intimate about being able to hold hands in the dark in a movie theatre with the girl of your dreams, while her head rests on your shoulder, her breath warming your neck at intervals. At times she would have a very normal human like reaction to the movie, such as gripping my hand tightly during a sudden jump scare. I remembered back in college that I had seen a comedy television programme where one of the lead characters doles out a piece of life advice to his friend, that horror movies were great aphrodisiacs. It seemed a very odd and outlandish statement to me at the time, but I could sense now that the statement had come from a place of experience and wisdom.

The highlight of the movie was the nostalgic theme music that brought back memories of childhood, the movie itself being a continuation of a franchise that had come into existence the year I was born.

We sat back in the movie theatre, listening to the theme music play out. I was slightly lost in the memories of having seen the previous instalments of the movie franchise in theatres with family members, and being wonderstruck as a kid, looking at the giant dinosaurs. Back then the dinosaurs were created out of functioning animatronics, as opposed to these days, when the studios rely on computer generated graphics to bring the monsters to life. The difference is quite noticeable and takes you out of the whole experience at times.

A short while later, one of the cleaners came in and began sweeping away popcorn and bits of nacho chips that had been crushed underfoot in the dark. I turned around and was surprised to see that Sandxira had dozed off with her head on my shoulder. I was not sure when it was that she had fallen asleep, but it was not that surprising either, considering everything that she had seen and experienced in the multiverse. Even a movie with stampeding dinosaurs would be unable to hold the unwavering attention of someone like Sandxira. It was like somebody, who had spent years at an underwater research facility, and seen creatures that most people could only dream of, being shown an aquarium and being asked to be wonderstruck at the fish that were swimming around in it.

I combed my hand through her hair. She made a pleasurable sound, and slowly opened her eyes, then jerked up and sat upright. The surroundings were unfamiliar to her; Sandxira had apparently forgotten that we were in a movie theatre.

"Thanks for not drooling." I said. Her hand instinctively reached up to her mouth. She was relieved to find that it was drool free, and smiled at me.

We walked out of the movie theatre, hand in hand and proceeded to the counter that sold the desserts that she liked. The salesperson at the counter tried aggressively to sell us on churros that had been newly launched by the dessert chain. Despite my aversion to cinnamon flavored food in general, I found the spiral nature of the rolls to be fascinating. It reminded me of a graphic novel that I had read a few years back about a mysterious curse in a small village that caused the residents to become obsessed and paranoid about spirals. One of the characters in the novel punctured her eardrum after finding out that the cochlea in the ear is shaped like a spiral. The curse culminated in physically turning everything, including people in the village, into spirals. It was a fascinating read at the time, although now it seemed a little pedestrian, considering everything that had transpired in the past few weeks. I narrated the gist of the graphic novel to Sandxira, after we picked up our desserts from the counter and started wading through the sea of tables in the mall food court, looking for a table to ourselves. The salesperson had failed in his sales pitch for churros. Sandxira was carrying a plate of cinnamon roll and I was carrying a chocolate pretzel and a cup of cappuccino coffee.

"Humans can really think up some bizarre things, despite being limited to existence in one universe, and one planet." Sandxira said, as we found a table and sat down perpendicular to each other.

"Can you guys travel to different time periods while phasing in and out of dimensions?" I asked.

"Theoretically that could be possible, but we have not yet discovered the ability to do so." Sandxira replied.

"Oh... Why do you say so?"

Sandxira had taken a big bite of the cinnamon roll in her excitement at having come to the mall after ages. She chewed on the piece, trying to figure out in her mind how best to explain it to me. She swallowed, her throat bobbed up and down and then she began.

"Imagine the multiverse as being layers of rubber lying on top of each other or next to each other, without leaving any space in between. Even though time flows differently in each universe, when we are trying to travel from one universe to another, we can only pass across the rubber membrane to the other side and reach a point in time that is corresponding to the point in time in that particular universe from when we left our universe. If we try to travel to a different time period, it would mean taking the dimensional membrane at a point of time in our universe and trying to get it to overlap with the dimensional membrane at a completely different point of time in the other universe. As you can imagine, this may give rise to a pocket universe, or lead to a discovery of a completely new underlying universe in itself. At present we do not have the technology, energy or knowledge to attempt such a feat, and we are also wary of what might lie in such pocket or unknown universes. It would be the equivalent of a conspiracy theorist of your universe trying to warn others against inter-dimensional travel in the first place, having no idea what such attempts might result in. Human history is full of works of fiction where such attempts have gone horribly wrong."

I was stirring my cup of coffee with one of those tiny plastic stirrers as I was mulled over what Sandxira just told me.

"Why do you ask?" Sandxira said.

"I was just curious, when you said that that humanity was limited to existence on one planet, whether, you or any of your peers have any idea about what lies in humanity's future, you know, whether we could end up becoming a space faring, planet colonizing species as romanticized in numerous works of science fiction."

She smiled.

"Maybe I will risk an invasion from the dungeon dimensions, look into humanity's future and let you know." She winked.

I leaned over and kissed her on the cheek.

"I have been meaning to talk to you about something." She said.

"What is it?"

"I need to go away for a while. I need to figure out what happened with my last phasing incident. But I may not want to risk phasing back anytime soon, till we can figure out what went wrong. It will be some time before I will be able to see you again."

"Oh... I see." I was unmindfully playing with my chocolate pretzel.

"Would you be okay with it?"

"Hmm...? Oh yes, of course. Please take as much time as you need. I will be here waiting."

"Thanks for understanding. This really has been unprecedented."

"Any ideas about what might have caused the incident?" I asked.

"Well, I confess that it was the first time that I was phasing in front of somebody, and not entirely by myself. It could have had something to do with the observer effect, that since you were observing me in that phenomenon, it inevitably changed that phenomenon."

"Layman's terms please." I requested.

"What I mean is, an object becomes visible to you after light falls on it and reflects back to your eye, so in effect, and this is in the simplistic terms, the object that is visible to your eye, may not be the exact same object as it existed independently, since the electrons in the object interacted with the photon that fell on the object, and got reflected back to your eye. Something similar could have happened in my phasing as well."

"Okay, so what you are saying is that I saw you by the act of light falling on you while you were phasing, light that got reflected back into my eyes, and that it could have interfered with your constituent particles when you were trying to go into resonance with the vibrations of your home universe, and such an incident could have disrupted the vibrations?" I asked.

"That is what may have happened, yes. Or it could have been an impact of information processing on space time." Sandxira replied.

"And that would be?"

"It is basically the fact that what conscious beings observe, can have an effect on space time. You as an observer set your limits on what can and cannot be reality, to the extent that only what your mind can perceive and believes to be reality is, in fact reality. That is why human beings cannot observe something such as a five dimensional space, and such space does not exist in the reality of your universe, because your brain in turn places a limitation on its existence. A conscious being's perception and the existence of the universe is a symbiotic process. The notion states that you do not discover physical laws about the universe but collaborate with the universe on them. Your theories are tested against past observations not only by yourself, but by the universe as well. If the universe agrees that past events are not contradicted by a theory, then that theory becomes a template and the universe goes along with it. The better a theory fits the facts, the longer it lasts. But the rules of the universe are not set in stone. An observer is shaping the very nature of the universe itself." Sandxira explained.

"So what you are saying is that by observing the very act of you phasing, which is not something that is consistent with the normal physical laws of this universe, the universe somehow rejected such an occurrence, especially since not enough people had observed and confirmed it to be part of a regular occurrence that might happen in this universe?"

"Yes, reality as perceived by the conscious mind is like an organism, and the universe correcting any anomalies to that organism is like the white blood cells in your body."

It had started to rain outside, fulfilling the prophecy that the gathering dark clouds of the evening seemed to have heralded. The fresh rain glistened on the panorama of towers and rooftops, unaware of the teeming and chaotic city that it was falling into. Luckier raindrops fell somewhat incestuously into the river. Rain that fell on the city was destined to be collected into puddles, muddled with dirt, and either be lucky enough to evaporate back into the air, or be flushed out with sewage through rat infested sewers.

We were about to take our empty plates and dump them in a steel dustbin, when one of the busboys standing around, stepped forward eagerly to collect them and clean up our table. Everyone had become eager to please and show sincerity in a slow economy. The only people immune to it, appeared to be the taxi drivers in the city, who were still whimsical about the fares that they wished to take. We finally managed to find one after being rejected by four taxis. Our messianic charioteer agreed to take us to Sandxira's home.

The rain had stopped by the time we got out of the mall. A cool wind was blowing, carrying remnants of rain drops and splashing people who had dared to venture out without their umbrellas. Sandxira and I sat down next to each other on the back seat. The window on the left hand side of the taxi was rolled down. I sat next to it with my right arm around Sandxira, as we pulled out of the taxi stand.

I began to comb my hand through her hair once again. She closed her eyes in ecstasy.

The city bore a busy look. The roads were filled with people travelling in their own vehicles or in taxis like us, to various places, trying to make the most of the weekend. We passed several restaurants with lit billboards that advertised various cuisines, both indigenous and foreign, exotic and generic. Nearly all restaurants were crowded with people, enjoying meals, having drinks with out of town friends, celebrating anniversaries and working on business pitches. In some places street urchins were playing with each other, waiting for the patrons to leave the restaurants so that the kids could run after them and beg for alms. Outside some establishments that were family restaurants, balloon sellers were waiting with their fares, hoping that some parent would give in to the demands of his or her kid and buy a balloon or some other toy from them. At other places, electronic showrooms, jewellery stores, liquor sellers, medicine retailers, sweet shops and other establishments selling various essential and non-essential goods, were open for business. The rain drenched neon speckled city looked like a painting of an avant garde artist, specializing in neo noir cyberpunk aesthetic.

"Do you want to go back home, or go somewhere else?" Sandxira asked.

"Do you have a place in mind?" I asked.

She pouted her lower lip indicating indecision.

"Well, you know Xeala and I often used to just cruise around the city in a taxi, just taking in the sights, wind blowing in our hair. I think I had told you about it. Would you want to do that?" I asked.

Her lower lip still pouted, she nodded, indicating assent.

I checked with our taxi driver, to see if he would be fine with our hare brained scheme. There was a time when taxi drivers in the city never asked questions or expressed dissatisfaction so long as the meters were running and they were getting paid. The entitlement had come later. We had been fortunate enough to be in the taxi of someone who was of the same spirit as those taxi drivers of yore, and our charioteer readily agreed to my suggestion. Mentally chalking out a route, I laid it out for him. The taxi driver was very familiar with the streets in the city, and caught on really fast. He pitched in with some excellent suggestions of his own, which would increase the efficiency of our tour, at the cost of lowering his revenue, but he seemed to be fine with it. He was an incredibly helpful person, or maybe the sight of the two of us in his backseat, brought back memories of his own younger days.

We took a detour, and passed through some of the less crowded roads of the city. We took the bypass that ran through the edge of the city, got up on an incredibly long flyover, which put us right next to the city race course. From there we took a right turn and passed through the wide roads of the financial districts with incredibly tall buildings on both sides of the road, standing guard over our procession. We turned left after a while, and passed by the ancient white cathedral where the whole city congregated on holidays. The cathedral had a gothic architectural style with sharp steeples that were pointed towards the sky like gargantuan white swords, daring invaders from the heavens to come down to the planet and disrupt our peace. Inside the cathedral was an impressive collection of stained glass wall paintings and frescoes, having been worked on by skilled painters during the colonial times. This city had been one of the most important trade and strategic centers in a bygone era. The weather rooster on top of one of the white steeples of the cathedral had been blown away by a storm, the previous year. Then we arrived at the city planetarium, a beige building with a marble dome on top of it. The planetarium housed an astronomy gallery that maintained a huge collection of fine paintings as well as celestial models created by renowned astronomers. It also had a state-of-the-art telescope, that was accessible for use by members of the public and students for astronomical projects and studies. Daily shows at the planetarium were conducted for amateur enthusiasts, which provided a brief synopsis of how the universe, as we knew it, came into existence. The show also provided fundamental details about the planets closest to us and the star that gave us life. The shows were projected onto the inside surface of the dome, which was a rough approximation of the extent of night sky visible to a person with the naked eye. The last show of the day had just gotten over and the visitors to the stars were coming out in throngs onto the rain soaked pavement, having missed most of the downpour during their interstellar voyage. A little way further from the planetarium put us next to the city museum. The museum was a white two storied incredibly huge colonial era building and had rare collections of antiques, armor and ornaments, fossils, skeletons, mummies and paintings. It had six sections comprising thirty five galleries of cultural and scientific artefacts. One of the star attractions of the museum, purely from an aesthetic viewpoint, was a large courtyard in the center of the building complex and a massive marble fountain in the middle of the courtyard. Benches were arranged in the courtyard for visitors to sit down on and rest when they got exhausted from roaming the unending labyrinth that was the museum. The place had closed nearly three hours ago, and the dark corridors were presently playing host to the restless undead, whose names are spoken of only in cautious whispers.

All of a sudden, we found ourselves close to the local cricket stadium. A few meters ahead was the river bank.

"Would you mind if we got down at the riverside?" Sandxira asked.

"Yes sure. I will ask him to stop when we reach." I said.

We got out of the car, when we reached our destination. I paid the driver some extra money for his troubles. He saluted me and drove off. We crossed the road, passed the familiar Palladian porch, and reached the river side. The embankment was in no position to be sat on that day. The rain had brought the dried up river mud back to life. Neither of us were feeling like sacrificing our clothes to the gods of laundry, so we decided to take a walk down the familiar, now drenched, cobblestone path. The boats had been docked early in anticipation of the storm that had passed. Some of the oarsmen were sitting in their boats and enjoying a quiet evening meal by the light of hurricane lamps. Snatches of songs from radio stations playing evergreen hits were audible, intermittently.

We had avoided talking about Sandxira's decision to go away for a while, to figure out what had gone wrong with her phasing. I had been planning to bring it up when we reached her home.

"When are you planning to go?" I asked.

"I was hoping I could leave day after tomorrow." Sandxira replied.

We walked for a few minutes in silence.

"I am scared." I confessed.

"Why?"

I reached out and took her hand.

"What if I lose you? What if you are unable to come back?"

Sandxira inched closer to me. We were still walking side by side.

"I am sorry." she said.

We continued to walk.

"Do you know when you may be back?" I asked.

"I cannot say that for sure, and it would be unfair of me to give you a false approxi-mation. I promise that I will come and see you the moment that I am able to phase back in."

"What if you never do?"

She did not have an answer for this.

"I do not want to be a burden for you, keep you unfairly tied to this universe, when you may be very well be done with it." I said.

"Are you saying you want to stop seeing me?" Sandxira asked.

"I do not want to. Apart from the fact that you are close to an incomprehensible cosmic entity, you are the most amazing person that I have ever met. Everything about you lights me up, your endearing smile, the way your hair always bunches up over your right shoulder, the way your lips feel when you kiss me, even when you are explaining incredibly complex ideas to me in layman's terms. Most of all, on days when I am with you, I wake up in the morning and cannot believe my luck that I get to be with someone like you. So no, I cannot bear the thought of breaking up with you, but I cannot be so selfish as to make you come back to this universe at great risk to your own existence. I know this makes me sound incredibly self-righteous, but please know that I am being sincere when I say this to you."

She squeezed my hand.

"I am not doing this for you. I am doing this for me. I want to be back here, I want to be with you. For that I need to understand what went wrong with my phasing. It is the only way I can avoid unpleasant incidents in the future. It is completely my decision, and you being here in this universe has no bearing on it, so please do not try to be a martyr." she said.

I looked at her and smiled weakly.

"For someone who claims to have read as much as you, you sure do speak sometimes in cliches." Sandxira teased me.

"Cliches are handy, they do the job. The reason that cliches become cliches is that they are the hammers and screwdrivers in the toolbox of communication." I said, quoting one of my favorite authors.

We stopped and turned to face each other. I held her face with my slightly cold hands and kissed her deeply. She reciprocated with enthusiasm. If I had been an animated character in a cartoon film, this would be around the time when the top of my head would be blown off.

We took a taxi back to her home. We could barely make it over the threshold of her flat without falling down, so entangled were we in each other. Later on, we laid in bed, her back to me, her head lying on my arm. Babies do not sleep this well.

~

I was awakened the next morning by the smell of fresh, hot tea. Sandxira had gotten up before me and made two cups. She had not bothered to put a robe on. Her un-clothed body was resplendent in the early morning sunlight that came in through the window, as she walked into the room and laid a steaming cup on the bedside table. The drapes on the window were waving slightly in an early morning breeze. By this point, we had given up any pretenses of wanting to be clothed around each other, especially after nights that we spent together.

I woke up with a grunt and realized that I had been snoring with my mouth open. I ran my tongue around the roof of my mouth, to moisten it before I could speak.

"Mmm... Good Morning" I said.

I ran my hand over my mouth, to wipe off flecks of drool that had slowly dripped through the night and soaked the pillow that I was sleeping on.

"Good morning" she said. She kissed me on the forehead and then on my lips. Maybe her sense of hygiene was starting to leave her, if she was willing to kiss me even with my horrendous morning breath.

"Sleep well?"

"Mmm..." I said, then pulled her by the hand and dragged her back in bed.

"So, I think I might try to phase out this morning, instead of tomorrow." Sandxira said after sometime, her leg across my stomach and her hand on my chest.

“Hmm... okay.” I turned towards her, and caressed her cheek with the back of my hand. She ran her fingers through my hair.

“Thanks for understanding.”

“Of course.” I said.

“I am going to go freshen up now and take a shower.”

“I will let myself out.” I said

“I was hoping that you would want to join me.”

“I would love to, but we have already been intimate, twice, since last night. I fear that it might interfere with your phasing.”

“As you wish. Let us take a rain check on it then.” Sandxira said

She stepped down from the bed, and began walking towards the washroom.

“Sandy?” I called back.

“Yeah?” she said as she turned around to look at me.

“I hate to see you go, but I love to watch you leave.”

PART 10: COUNSEL OF THE WISE

It had been a week since Sandxira left. I was not sure when she would be coming back. This was one of the hazards of an inter-dimensional relationship. There is no way to check up on the other person. The technology to do so has either not been invented, or even if it has, the use of such technology by my fragile human brain could very well break my mind and shatter my psyche.

I tried to stay upbeat for Sandxira's sake for the first few days, but I was starting to get worried. Time flowed differently in her dimension, but I had failed to ask her how different exactly. For all I knew, years could have passed in her universe, or maybe it had just been hours. I slowly found myself sinking into the habit of listening to hours of endless songs about pining for someone who has gone far away, but whose return is eagerly awaited. The discography on this subject was quite fertile, and Metallica's 'Nothing Else Matters' led the way, from the front.

The nature of Sandxira's phasing trouble would require some in depth analysis and would take time, but I was getting restless. I mean what is the point of becoming a multiverse hopping race of beings, if you still have not worked out the quantum mechanics related kinks? Damn the universe's physical laws and its symbiotic relationship with the human consciousness.

Thankfully Xeala was there to keep my spirits up. When I had told her over the phone of what had transpired between Sandxira and I, she had positively squealed. I had to hold my phone away at arm's length, afraid that it might explode.

"This is amazing!" she exclaimed.

"Thank you, thank you." I said, a little abashed.

"How did it happen?"

I told her in detail about the sequence of events that had transpired, from the evening walk in the university, to hanging out at the river side, to the boat ride across the river, and finally spending the night together. Xeala was eager for specifics, so I had to describe through lurid narration, the events that transpired that night between Sandxira and I. By the end, it appeared that if it was physically possible, Xeala would stick her hand down her phone and use it to punch me on the shoulder when her hand came out on my side, calling me a dawg, spelt with an 'a' and a 'w'. It was not that Xeala was a tomboyish girl, or used masculinity as a shield. It's just that we were incredibly close and had no hesitation in being ribald with each other. She was quite a feminine girl, who liked to dress well, treat herself to the finer things in life and spent hours browsing through ethnic wear shops, trying to find the perfect gift for someone.

I had carefully avoided telling Xeala about the fact that Sandxira was from a different reality and was possibly an ancient cosmic entity chronicling human lives. Xeala already had little patience with me because of my tendency to drop more popular culture references in a single conversation with her, than most normal people did in their entire lifetimes, except for maybe someone like Abed Nadir who was raised by a television and a cable connection. My habit had started out inadvertently, but had snowballed and gone out of control when I realized how annoyed Xeala got sometimes with my references. However, confessing something as seemingly outlandish like Sandxira's true nature, would be the icing on the cake of my attempts to vex Xeala. Besides, it was not my story to tell. It was Sandxira's only. She had trusted me with her secret, and I wanted to respect that trust. I had to make up a story about Sandxira being called off for work to some remote place that was beyond the reach of mobile networks or any other conventional means of communication. It was a hard sell, but Xeala seemed to buy it.

"I can understand. Do not worry, she will be fine. You said that she would only be gone for a few weeks, right?" Xeala asked.

"I hope so. She could not tell me the nature of her assignment. Apparently, there are confidentiality restrictions, so I do not know when she will be back exactly, to be honest." I was making it up as I went along.

"Did she at least tell you where she was going?"

"She did, but asked me not to tell anyone. I am sorry Xeala."

"Fair enough. Why don't you land up there without telling her and surprise her?"

"If only I could. Work pressure has picked up in office and my deliverables are getting out of hand. Almost every client has woken up all of a sudden and are demanding that we prioritize their work. It is worse than a zombie apocalypse, since the zombies at least have the decency to eat your brain outright, instead of chewing on it piecemeal. Not sure if I will be able to take leave at a short notice." I was sprinting now.

"Hmm... Too bad."

"Let me figure something out." I said.

"Can you send her something such as a care package? Do you have like an address? Maybe you can ask a friend or colleague of hers from office. Maybe that girl with the inter faith marriage."

"Worst title for a Stieg Larsson book, but that is a good idea. Let me work on it."

"Great! Let me know how it goes!"

"This why you still are my number one girl." I said. Unfortunately, it was the first honest and true thing that I had said to Xeala in the past few minutes.

She laughed. "Are you sure Sandxira has not taken the spot yet?" She asked.

"No one can." If we had been texting, I would have followed this with a smiling face emoji and emoji sporting an angelic band.

"So how is it going with Axxen?" I asked.

"It has been going really well. He tries to visit me every alternate month and after he leaves, I have to call the carpenter to fix the fittings of my bed." Xeala said in a deadpan voice.

"Thank you for that image." I said sarcastically.

"On a serious note. I have been really happy with him. He has always been so patient with me, he never loses his temper with me even when I am being unreasonable and whimsical. It is too early to say yet, fingers crossed, but he might be the one."

"Damn..." the one that I let out was considerably longer, than is permitted to be depicted, by good grammar sense, in the written medium.

"In fact, last week we had gone to..." and Xeala proceeded to tell me the story of a weekend gateway trip that she and Axxen had taken to an ancient city in the southern part of the country that was close to Axxen's place of work. The city was on a hilly terrain formed by granite boulders. The place used to be an ancient pilgrimage center and was once an incredibly wealthy, prosperous and grand city in the past. At present, the city housed perfectly preserved amazing ruins of architectural interest, including forts, riverside features, royal courtyards, shrines, pillared halls and memorial structures. The place had been painfully preserved and maintained by the country's Archaeological Society. Despite being a major tourist attraction, visitors to the place were quite respectful of the sites. Maybe they were in awe of the ancient monuments that stood before them, having weathered the unkind years, and borne witness to the progress of civilization. Nevertheless, the place had a peaceful quality to it, that made it quite alluring to couples looking for a short trip away from the city to get away from all the hustle and bustle.

"So, did you guys run around the ancient pillars and serenade each other with songs, like in the old movies?" I teased.

"Shut up." Xeala said. She would have punched me through the phone again, if it was possible.

"Did you cross paths with any ancient undead priests, like Imhotep, who offered his services to marry you guys off?"

"No..." there was a hesitation in Xeala's voice.

"Xeala?"

"What?"

"Tell me."

"Honestly, I was kind of hoping, that Axxen would be popping the question during this trip." said Xeala, "We have been together for nearly four years now and even though things are great, sometimes I do not know if this is what I want, to be in a relationship without any direction."

"Had Axxen said something to you, that made you think that he was going to propose?"

"He has been extra sweet and caring recently."

"Isn't that like second nature to him?"

"I may have read the signals wrong."

"Hmm... it would be quite amazing to get some good news now."

"This may sound like I am conforming to the stereotypes, but at this point, I really do not want to feel like I have wasted my time with Axxen. It was okay to date someone and fool around without thinking about the future when we were younger, and not have any hang ups. But at present both of us have been invested in this relationship for a little over three years, and it would be a pain to start things all over again with someone else, if this does not work out." Xeala confessed.

"Why don't you say something to him? In fact, why do you not pop the question to him, if you think he is the right person?" I asked.

"I am scared. What if he freaks out?"

"If he does, it will be his loss, for losing out on the opportunity of spending his life with this amazing girl."

"You are just flattering me."

"I am not Xeala. You are like the girl Eric Clapton sang about in 'Layla'. You deserve to have people go crazy about you. And you know I am not being a prick when I say all this, because I find it incredibly hard to fake sincerity and cannot say anything positive about anyone unless I really mean it."

"I love you. I wish you were here right now."

"I love you too."

We shared a moment of silence.

"Do not worry about this. Hopefully things will be fine. Axxen will do the right thing, whether he pops the question or you do. He is a gem of a person." I said.

"Thanks. I miss you so much."

"I miss you as well."

"Who says 'as well' idiot? Are you writing an inter-office memo or something?"

"It's good to have you back."

~

It was three days after the chat with Xeala that my phone lit up. I was at work, and had put my phone inside a drawer next to my desk. I had taken to frequently checking my phone for any messages from the other side. As evident, this was a major impediment at work, and I kept losing my train of thought.

That day I was determined to not let the phone distract me and it was not until lunch hour that I took it out from the drawer to check it. When the screen lit up, I was elated. There was a single missed call from Sandxira. There was a message too. It just had one word; "Hi".

Surging with excitement, I walked to the front door of the office and punched my index finger into the biometric scanner, a little harder than I meant to. It earned me a wrathful glare from the office receptionist. The lock opened with a beep and I hurriedly walked out through the swinging glass doors of the office without a backward glance or even a perfunctory apology to Sauron's eye. When I reached the stairwell next to the fire escape, I dialed Sandxira's number.

"Hi." she came on the other side.

"Hi! Hi!" I said. I was breathless and my voice was shaking with excitement. I was barely able to stand without feeling that my knees would buckle under me at any moment.

"What's up?" she asked.

I had sat down on the stairs. My heart was thumping loudly in my chest. I bit down on my knuckles to stay calm.

We were silent on the line, while I waited to calm down.

"It is so good to hear your voice." There was still a tremor in my voice as I spoke.

"As is yours. I have missed you so much. It was eons back home."

"I missed you too," I said, not willing to fall back into the same trap as with Xeala.

"Are you in office?"

"Yes I am. Where are you?"

"I am back at my place."

"Is everything okay? What about your office?"

"I do not know yet. You are first one I tried to get in touch with, once I came back." Sandxira said.

"How are you feeling?" I had missed asking the most important question.

"Not great to be honest. Phasing back took a toll."

"I am so sorry. Do you want me to come over?"

"It is okay. Do not stress yourself. Can we meet in the evening tomorrow?"

"Of course," I said, "Wherever you want me to be, I will be there."

"Great. Can we meet at the grounds opposite my office building?"

"'We can for sure. I will be there."

"Thanks." Sandxira said.

"Is everything okay? Will you be fine by yourself?"

"Yes, yes. I just need to figure some things out. I will see you tomorrow then."

"Great."

It was not exactly the reunion that I had hoped for. Despite Sandxira's assurances, I felt an ominous trepidation. Things had probably not gone as she had expected them to. She appeared a little distant over the phone.

Feeling a little deflated, I went back to my desk, and sat down looking absentmindedly at the computer monitor. I was supposed to have been working on a draft petition for an upcoming trade mark dispute, but I did not feel up to it at the moment. It was quite an unprofessional attitude to adopt, I later reflected, but sometimes it is incredibly difficult to separate your personal life from your professional life. I was falling back into the same pattern as before.

The rest of the lunch time was quite underwhelming as well, as I sat in silence at my desk, brooding. One of my work friends, Natascha, came over and asked me to join her for lunch.

"I am not feeling up to it. Sorry. Please carry on." I said politely.

"Are you sure?" Natascha asked.

"Yes."

"You look stressed out."

"I just got some troubling news, trying to process it."

"Oh... Okay... Please make sure that you eat sometime," Natascha said, "you should not be skipping meals."

"Will do." I said and smiled at her.

Natascha was a caring person; very cheerful and extroverted. She was one of the few likeable people in the office, who genuinely wanted to be your friend, and did not have any ulterior motive.

"I hope you feel better soon. Let me know if you want to talk." she said.

I smiled again, and made a half bowing motion. Natascha turned away and walked towards the cafeteria, her hair was open and was swinging from left to right. She had a tendency to walk on her toes, which gave off the impression that she perpetually had a spring in her step. Her infectious and effervescent personality seemed to corroborate that.

~

In the evening I messaged Xeala and told her that Sandxira was back. When she messaged me asking about it, not feeling like typing in detail, I dialed her number. She disconnected the call, but dialed back half an hour later.

"Sorry, was speaking to the landlord. He has been bothering us about increasing the rent, and we are trying to get him to put it off till the beginning of the next year." she explained. Xeala shared her flat with two other women, one of whom worked in a public relations firm, and the other one worked in a bank.

"Was he convinced?" I asked.

"It is an ongoing negotiation. We have reached a deadlock at present, but hope to make headway soon."

"That is great."

"So, tell me, what happened with Sandxira?" Xeala asked.

"It was fine. A little strange to be honest. She seemed stressed, so I asked her if she wanted me to come over, but she said that she was fine and asked if we can meet tomorrow at the grounds opposite her office building. She said that she needed to figure some things out."

And involuntary "*Yeash*" escaped from Xeala.

"Huh?" I asked.

"Sorry, that did not mean anything." Xeala tried to cover up.

"What was the Yeash about?"

"It may be nothing, I might be misconstruing it for all I know."

"What are you misconstruing?"

"Do not hate me for this, but it kind of sounds like Sandxira wants to ends things with you."

"Oh... What makes you say that?" I asked.

"Well... saying that she is fine when she is clearly stressed, not wanting you to come over, saying that she needs to figure things out, asking you to meet her in a public place, so that the chances of creating a scene is minimized, these are all red flags, buddy. These are what I would say when I want to break up with someone, and trust me, I *have* said these to people that I have broken up with."

"Ugh...Damn it Xeala! Why do you have to be so perceptive?" I said in a frustrated tone.

"I am sorry, I do not know what else to say, but I really do hope that everything is fine, and whatever it is that is bothering her, may not be caused by you, or because of you."

"Hmm..." I let out a long sigh.

"At least think about it this way," Xeala persisted, "now that you are forewarned, even if she does break up with you, you will not be blindsided. You will be able to deal with it in a better manner."

"Remind me to never let you tell me that I have cancer."

"Asshole." she said.

~

The next day I took leave from work. Xeala's seemingly perceptive conclusions, about the hidden meaning of Sandxira's words, had been reassuring to an extent, but it meant that I would be unable to focus on anything till I met Sandxira in the evening and found out for myself what it was that she wanted to talk about.

I laid the entire day on my bed, looking up at the ceiling. I was not really thinking anything, but somehow found the completely white featureless flat surface fascinating.

I watched the progress of a common house gecko, that was hanging upside down, slowly stalking its prey. It was a fly that had somehow managed to come in and had settled on the ceiling, trying to decide which place in the room smelt the most inviting so that it could fly over and perch there next. The gecko crawled towards the un-mindful fly at a glacial pace, till it was mere inches from it. The fly, having arrived in a completely new home, was observing its surroundings with fascination, much as an astronaut does, when he or she lands on a new planet, becoming engrossed with the place's indigenous flora and fauna. I watched in morbid fascination as the gecko shot out its long sticky tongue and grabbed the fly. The gecko pulled its prey back into its mouth, and then clamped its jaws shut, crushing the fly between them. The legs of the fly thrashed about in the last throes of death, before going limp. The gecko continued to stand still in place, making sure that the fly was dead. Only when it was convinced, did it slowly began moving its jaws, and crawled away from the place of the hunt.

I slowly got up from my bed, took a shower, and got dressed. Then I stood in front of the mirror looking at myself.

"Its fine. You will be fine." I said to the mirror.

"What can you do?" My reflection shrugged back at me.

"It was only a matter of time." I consoled my reflection.

"You probably won't feel the same way about anyone ever again."

"Yeah, you may be in love again, but being in love will never feel the same way to you, as it did when you were with her."

"You will just have to learn to deal with it."

"And respect her decision."

"Yes, that too."

"By the way, did you hear the joke about the guy whose rear-view mirror fell off and he never fixed it?"

"No, I did not." I confessed

"He has not looked back since."

~

I was in a trance as I took the bus to Sandxira's office. It was the kind of trance shown in avant garde music videos shot through SnorriCams, which are nausea inducing at times, with their frenetic pace and their attempts to present a dynamic point of view from the actors' perspective, giving the appearance that they are standing steady but everything around them is moving. It creates an odd and unusual sense of vertigo.

The conductor on the bus had to call me twice and tap me on the shoulder before I realized that he was standing next to me expectantly, waiting for me to purchase the ticket. I was not carrying my earphones that day, but did not seem to be disturbed by the cacophony of the traffic on the streets. I had other things to occupy my mind.

I reached Sandxira's office sometime later, got down from the bus, and messaged her, letting her know that I had arrived. Then I proceeded to stroll to the grounds next to the bus stop where I had been dropped off.

Evening was approaching, and the usual crowds of visitors to the grounds were starting to gather. Various vendors of street food had set up their stalls in anticipation of substantial evening sales, courtesy of the tourists and other regular patrons. The fares on sale included sweetmeats, momos, roasted potatoes tossed in thick gravy, various kinds of stuffed and regular flatbreads, spicy puffed rice mixtures, and an assortment of fritters.

The wind had picked up, blowing the incredible medley of smells from the stalls towards me. For a brief moment I forgot about Sandxira and realized that I had not eaten anything since the morning. I found myself almost floating in the air towards the food stalls, being drawn by the enticing smells. As I was finishing up a piping hot plate of momos, my phone buzzed with Sandxira's message, "I am out of office, where are you?"

I turned towards her office building that was visible on the other side of the road and saw Sandxira standing on the pavement. She was wearing a white blouse that day, with black trousers and a grey coat. In my hurry to finish eating, I wolfed down the last piece of momo, misjudging exactly how hot the chicken filling was inside, which systematically proceeded to blister my tongue, and burn my esophagus as it went down. In pain I stamped on the ground, hoping that it would make the discomfort go away, and quickly gulped down water from a jug that was handed to me by the alarmed proprietor of the momo shop. Finally, having calmed down the raging fire inside me, I took a brief pause and then I proceeded to cross the road to go over to Sandxira. I noticed that she was trying to stop herself from laughing, her hand tightly clamped over her mouth. Evidently my antics had the trappings of classic slapstick comedy.

"Hi" I said, as I reached her.

She threw her arms around me and buried her face in my chest. We stood there standing in the street for an entire fifteen seconds. Towards the end I could not figure out what else to do with my hands, so I proceeded to pat her a little awkwardly on the back and then rubbed her shoulders. After a while, she finally let go.

"I have missed you." Sandxira said.

"I have missed you as well."

She smiled and kissed me.

"What's up?" I asked

"Let's take a walk." she said, and held on to my hand.

"So how did it go?" I asked.

"Not exactly as I was hoping it would be." Sandxira replied.

"How long were you there?"

"Nearly a year, of our time."

"Ah..." I could not think of anything else to say, and "woah" seemed to be overdone and repetitive.

We walked for some time in silence. The footpaths had started to teem with people who were either getting out of offices or taking an evening break to have some tea or smoke cigarettes. The air was starting to smell overwhelmingly of burnt tobacco. I had developed an aversion to tobacco smoke since giving up cigarettes myself and becoming a convert to the non-smoker's club. As a result, I was trying harder than the regular members of the club to fit in and pledge my allegiance to the cause, and as a result was quick to be offended by even the slightest whiff of cigarettes.

We turned into a lane after walking for some time, which was mainly reserved for pedestrian traffic and did not have the blaring noises of cars or buses to interrupt conversations.

"So, what happened? Did the phasing not go seamless?" I asked.

"It did not."

"Why?"

"Because of you." Sandxira said.

"Me?" I was flabbergasted.

"And because of oxytocin and the limitations of this body."

"I do not follow."

She turned to me and said, "Oxytocin is a hormone that is produced by the female body."

"I vaguely seem to have read that in biology class sometime."

"It is a hormone that is associated with human emotions like empathy, trust, sexual activity and relationship building. It usually increases during activities such as hugging or lovemaking."

"Okay."

"When we had researched and designed this form for me to be able to phase into when I come into your universe, we tried to make it as anatomically correct as possible, in order for me to blend in. This extended to ensuring a hormonal balance in the body. Oxytocin is produced in the hypothalamus of this body that you see before you and is transported and secreted by the pituitary gland at the base of the brain."

"So, you are saying that you are susceptible to human emotions?" I asked.

"To an extent yes. This means that we bleed when we are cut, we are susceptible to headaches and body pains, we get sexually aroused, we get hungry, we feel sleepy and for all intents and purposes, for the time being that we are in this universe, we are mortal."

"So, can you be injured if you are struck by a car, or by something as pedestrian as throwing out your back while lifting weights?" I asked.

"Yes. When we are phasing out of this universe or any universe for that matter, we need to ensure that the chemical composition of our bodies is in order and exactly the same as it was when we had phased in. This means that if we had designed a body that had low production of insulin, for any of us to phase into, we would need to ensure that the insulin level stayed exactly the same when that someone phased out. This helped us avoid temptation and undertake any activity that could potentially alter the chemical composition of our bodies, like getting inebriated. It ensured that we could continue to remain passive observers without being entangled in the lives of the people that we were supposed to be observing. That is why I had to refuse when you asked me out the first time. That and the fact that I did not know if it could work between us. But our continued chats over messages and meeting you later when you came back to the city, changed all that." Sandxira said.

"It did?"

"For the first time, I did not feel like being a passive observer. I wanted to know you, wanted to be with you, wanted to be entangled in your life, wanted to be intimate with you. I found you alluring. And that messed everything up."

"I am sorry." I said.

"Do not be, this is not your fault. Every time we were intimate, when we kissed, when we made love, this body that I am in, released oxytocin. It continued to alter the chemical composition of this body without me consciously realizing it, because I was so caught up with you and so lost we were in each other. The first time I tried phasing in front of you, my blood had a higher content of oxytocin than it was supposed to, so when I phased out, the body that left this universe and went to the other was not the same that had phased in, and this caused the phasing anomaly, because my universe did not recognize the form that was coming back into it."

"But you came back successfully the first time, it was only the second time that the anomaly occurred."

"Like the human body that initially stumbles when it is first faced with an infection, the universe had failed to notice it at first, as it had occurred like an incredibly minor blip, but by the time I phased back in the second instance, the universe had taken note of the anomaly and was trying its best to correct it."

"Wait, so if I understand this correctly, you had effectively become an infection to your universe?"

"Yes. My theory on impact of information processing on space time having affected me was correct, except the space time I was thinking about was not your universe, it was mine. The observers in my universe had set their limits on what they could and could not perceive as reality. The universe disagreed with my presence there, based on past phasing that had occurred till then, where the travelers had gone away and come back as the same entity. However, since my occurrence was such an isolated incident, it did not comply with the physical laws of my universe, and my existence was rejected. This is why I could not achieve resonance and subsequently adopt the vibrations of my universe. This is why I still appeared fractured to you when I came back to this universe the second time."

All this was too much information. I found a bench by the side of the street, and sat down, my hands cupping my face, trying to make sense of it all. Sandxira sat down beside me and put a hand on my shoulder.

"But then, the day when you said that you would be phasing back to return to your universe, the night before that, we had been intimate." I said.

"I did not phase that day. I had to wait an entire day, calm myself, get myself to stop thinking about you, wait for the oxytocin levels to normalize and then attempt the phasing. I had a slight suspicion that this was the case even back then, but was not sure of its accuracy, so I did not say anything to you, except for off handedly discussing some elemental points of my suspicion with you. But now when I went back, I thoroughly researched on it and tried to find a way around it, tried consulting the best available minds on it, but it seems that till date we have not found a way around this problem of incorporating chemical changes of our alter-universe forms into our phasing.”

By now my hands had moved up to my eyes, and I was rubbing them slowly and deliberately, unmindfully looking at the orange spots that formed over the darkness of my closed eyelids.

We sat in silence for a while. I was sitting hunched over and she was leaning against me with a hand on my shoulder, her chin resting on the back of her hand.

“To be honest, I kind of see where we may need to go with this. I am not as surprised as I was expecting to be.” I said.

Sandxira looked at me and smiled sadly.

“We need to talk about this.” She said.

“I know” I said, feeling deflated.

“I am sorry.”

“Its fine. Right about now I would say something pretentious or contemplative about this being the intention of some higher power in the universe, but that would be disrespectful to you, and whatever decision you come to.”

“Can we talk this over tomorrow?” She asked.

“Fair enough.”

We sat on that bench holding hands, till evening gave way to twilight, which finally became night. I walked her to her home, kissed her on the cheek, turned around and began walking away.

I got back home and messaged Xeala, "It went better than expected, although the outcome might still be as you predicted." Then I put my phone on silent mode and laid down on my bed.

I woke up in the morning to find five missed calls from Xeala on my phone.

PART 11: DRINKS IN A SPACESHIP

We were sitting at a coffee shop close to Sandxira's office. Our table was next to one of the massive plate glass windows that looked out onto the street outside. Our view was obstructed in places by the name of the shop. The place had a heritage of nearly ninety years, but had managed to retain its quality and ambience through the changing times, adapting ever so slightly, and relying on the nostalgia of customers as well as positive word of mouth buzz to stay in business. The place had catered to us, our fathers before us and to their fathers before them. It was very difficult to find an indigenous home-grown coffee shop that could still compete with the chain based coffee shops, even though the latter were rarely good. There were exceptions like Lo Scoglio to be fair, which was part of a chain but served really good coffee and food. But in terms of being able to consistently maintain high quality, most of them were ticking time bombs.

It was oddly surreal to see people walking up and down the street outside or passing by in cars and buses, each of them with their own concerns and worries, a lot of them maybe under the egoistical assumption that they are the center of the universe and nothing else mattered, blissfully unaware of their own insignificance. It must have been incredibly comfortable for them to live in ignorance and to not know how utterly meaningless and fleeting they were compared to all of reality.

Sandxira and I walked in and placed our order with the cheerful hair mitten and apron wearing cashier, who greeted us with an enthusiastic "Good Morning". Then we proceeded to find a table and sat down, waiting for our order to be ready. The coffee shop was quite big inside and had the decor of an old timey movie theatre. Some of the fittings may have been actually procured from movie theatres going out of business I pondered, like the massive chandelier that hung in the middle of the shop. Even the cutlery had a vintage feel to it, being made of brass rather than stainless steel.

I ordered a plateful of breakfast foods with a black coffee, and Sandxira ordered an open Swiss sandwich and a watermelon juice. After a ten minute wait, a smiling waiter came over to our table, his arms cradled with plates of our food. The employee benefits at this place must be excellent, I mused, for the staff to always be ready to draw back their lips and flash their blinding smiles. Basuretta would easily fit into a place like this.

I was mesmerized by the enticing smell when the waiter put my plate down in front of me. Aesthetically plated on it was two rashes of crispy bacon, grilled pork sausages, poached eggs, a grilled tomato, mushroom tossed in spinach and one single crispy golden brown flat piece of hash brown. In front of Sandxira, the waiter set down her open Swiss sandwich. I had never seen something that was such a unique preparation. On a slab of toasted oatmeal bread was laid down a bed of lettuce, and on it was piled shredded chicken, some slices of ham, a few slices of tomato, pickles and two slices of cheese. An egg fried sunny side up was gently placed on top to finish off the ensemble. Turning to the table next to us, I noticed that the patron had ordered the exact same dish, but his had one slice of cheese instead of two.

"It seems that the waiter has a crush on you." I said.

"Oh, is it?" Sandxira seemed surprised.

"Either that or he has messed up your order and accidentally added an extra slice of cheese."

She gave a light laugh, turned halfway in her chair and waved to the waiter, mouthing "Thank you". The waiter seemed to blush and waved back.

"Bon Appetit" I said.

"Bon Appetit" Sandxira echoed, and we proceeded to dig in.

We had come into the shop to talk, but neither of us seemed keen to take the initiative to start the conversation. It was the whole Schrödinger's cat conundrum once again. Till we actually said anything to each other, we could continue to be absolutely fine, or be in problematic situation both at the same time. Only by one of us speaking out loud could the situation physically manifest itself, and help us reach a definitive conclusion. We were hoping to put it off for as long as we could, but time was not on our side. I decided that I had to say something after we finished eating.

My bacon strips were quite good. They were not too thick, which tended to make them chewy, and were fried perfectly to have just the right amount of crispiness without losing the flavor. The sausages were nothing to write home about, the grilled tomato was perfunctory as well, and the eggs were good too, but the real star of the plate was the mushroom tossed in spinach. The mushroom had a really strong flavor, which was effectively undercut by the spinach, but it was still a sensory overload for the taste buds. I had blistered my tongue the previous evening, but could still taste a lot of flavor coming from the mushroom. Sandxira sat opposite me and took small bites out of her sandwich. She intermittently sipped on her watermelon juice. Sandxira had been smart and taken the egg off the top of the sandwich, put it in the middle, and inverted the ham and cheese layer, so that the ham on top became the upper bun of the sandwich. She then proceeded to dig in. I had sampled some of the sandwich as well, and it was amazing. Sandxira had excellent choice in food.

Sandxira's form was like a machine, she had told me. It needed fuel in the form of food to be able to function effectively. "When we do happen to get injured," she had said, "in the few fractions of a second between the harm occurring and its manifestation in physical stimulus as pain, we can phase out of this universe, which allows the form to recuperate without any changes to its chemical composition. It is like being placed in an induced coma."

We continued to eat in relative silence, taking small bites out of our food and making them last as long as possible, to put off the discussion.

"How is the food?" I asked.

"It is quite nice. I cannot believe that I have been here for two years with this coffee shop so close to my apartment, and this is the first time I have come here. This place is definitely going in my chronicles."

"I wonder how the owners will feel when they find out that they listed are on inter-dimensional Yelp." I said.

"Food connoisseurs of the multiverse are a lot less cruel and critical. That much I can assure you." Sandxira said.

"I am glad that you like this place so much." I said, "I was wondering if I could read some of these chronicles that you keep mentioning."

"Well, to be fair, the chronicles are not maintained in what you may perceive in this universe as paper or even computers records. They are weaved into the fabric of our reality, designed so that any life form that discovers a way to safely travel to our universe, will be able to observe them in the form that such beings are accustomed to process information. I cannot physically take you to my universe as your body will not be able to handle the phasing. It is really difficult to predict how your body will reach there, in definitive terms, but there is a good chance that you may very well be shredded to an atomic scale and then dissipate."

"That seems about right," I said, through a mouthful of sausages.

"And any chronicles that I might try and bring back would be unstable in this universe. They would dissipate, much like the fruit that I showed you the other day."

"Even with proper phasing clearance?" I asked.

"Such sensitive information will not be able to go through phasing clearance in the first place."

"Would not want to do that either. The lost data might have helped some inter-dimensional traveler escape the clutches of an octopus faced bat winged lion god," I said, "but I have to say, that for a seemingly altruistic race of dimension hoppers, your bureaucrats seem to be mighty precious about the very object of their altruism; knowledge."

She laughed. I would have kissed her if I did not have chewed up food in my mouth.

"Would you like to order anything else?" I asked, as I wiped the last dregs of egg yolk with a piece of hash brown.

"I am good, but I would not mind sharing a chicken croissant with you."

I hailed the smiling water and placed an order for the same. "And bring us a plate of sunshine and rainbows too, while you are at it," I was tempted to say.

The croissant arrived almost immediately, a tray of them having been freshly baked and put out for the breakfast crowd. It was surprisingly good. My previous experiences with croissants had been middling, but the combination of shredded chicken, mayonnaise and mustard inside a flaky pastry, that was just lightly crisp and salty, somehow worked brilliantly.

All in all, it seemed to be a good beginning to the day.

The great thing about the coffee shop was that you could laze around after you had finished your meal. You were never ushered out by a waiter carrying your bill to the table. You could pay when you were ready. The proprietors of the establishment wanted to provide customers with a relaxed and holistic ambience. The place had sufficient number of tables to accommodate patrons, and yet never felt crowded. There was not much rush in the morning anyway, when we were seated in the coffee shop.

As we finished eating, I plucked out a couple of tissue papers, wiped my face, crumpled them up and dropped them on my plate. Sandxira followed suit, and a busboy dutifully came forward, picked up the plates and took them back to the kitchen.

I plucked out another tissue paper and began tearing it up into small pieces, absentmindedly. I was not sure how to broach our discussion. I had run scenarios of it could go in my head, but when the time had come to actually have the talk, I found myself unable to figure out how or where to start.

"What have you decided?" I asked.

"About?"

"What to order for dessert?"

Sandxira shook her head and laughed.

"Wait, let me rewind." I said, and made a sound like being a tape being turned backwards.

"About staying back in this universe or going back to yours?" I asked.

She leaned forward with her elbows on the table, her index fingers massaging the bridge of her nose, as if she was lost deep in thought.

"If we are together, this body will continue to act like a human body does. It will continue to produce oxytocin and alter its inherent chemical composition, as we keep getting intimate, and I find myself falling harder and harder for you. There will come a time when even abstinence will not work, and the chemical composition of this body will be irreversibly changed. I will never be able to go back if that happens. I will be stuck here forever, having to live out my days till the eventual end." Sandxira said.

"It may not be the worst thing." I whispered.

"It may not be, but I feel that I have a larger obligation and purpose. I am afraid that it will not be possible to have one without the other. As long as we are together, I will never be able to phase properly, or continue to make my chronicles. I barely managed to phase the last couple of times. Who knows what will happen if I attempt to do so now? What I fear would happen to you during phasing, might end up happening to me, or I might find myself stuck in one of the intermediary pocket dimensions or underlying universes, and never be able to go back to mine, or come back to yours. I would be like a ghost stuck between two worlds, unable to move on to the afterlife, and unable to connect with the ones it has left behind."

I sat with my hand covering my eyes.

"I feel that it would be the right decision to leave." Sandxira said.

I put my elbow on the table, my mouth resting on my knuckle, and looked out of the shop window. We sat in silence for some time.

"What if you manage to figure out a way to incorporate chemical changes of your alter-universe forms into your phasing?"

Sandxira looked at me sadly. "That is not going to happen for a while," she said, "we are still not at that stage of technological advancement. Even if we do find a way to incorporate such changes and create a stable alter-universe form, it would be ages before that happens. You may be long gone from this universe by then."

I let out a long drawn out sigh and then sat in silence for some more time. My head was pounding. It was harder to come to terms with our predicament than I had expected it to be. I felt truly helpless, but there was nothing that I could do.

"I understand." I finally said, "Honestly I was hoping that it would not amount to this, that there could be a way by which I could make you stay back, change your mind, but I know that is not going to happen."

"I am sorry."

"What happens if you decide to stay back in this universe? Forever?"

"I do not know for sure, but probably my body will continue to get old and decay, and then eventually if I die here, I will cease to exist as an entity either in this universe or in my own." she said.

"What about your consciousness?"

"Alas, for all our advancements, even we have not been able to figure out if there exists any afterlife at all."

I sighed. "It may not be the worst thing to remain mortal." I said.

"A human being's existence is fleeting in the scheme of this," Sandxira gestured towards herself and towards me, "and in comparison to all universes out there." Sandxira said.

"We have so many things to offer. Love, empathy, determination, courage. We are a foolhardy species and tend to run into walls with blind confidence, hoping for the wall to crumble. Our mortality is always a reminder to us to appreciate the things that we do have and not take them for granted, for those which are most precious to us may be taken away from us some day. We may be singularly focused on our ambitions, but every once in a while, we meet someone who takes our breath away, and makes us throw away all our hard work, just to be able to spend one more moment with that person. We are not ashamed to make a fool of ourselves when we meet that special someone." I said.

"You make a compelling argument," she smiled. I could sense that she was trying to placate me, but I was not about to give up.

"Oh, and food has become a lot better. We have hundreds of streaming services over the world wide web and near unlimited content to choose from for your viewing pleasure. There is enough literature to keep you occupied for the rest of your life as a mortal. Sports tournaments are great for the excitement that you may be looking for. Jobs are good too, you know, to keep you distracted. Dates like these also take up a lot of your time."

She reached out for my hand, and held it tightly.

"Its fine." I said, patting her hand, "This is probably the hardest thing that I will ever have to come to terms with."

I leaned back on my chair, resting the back of my hand on my forehead. Then I leaned forward and shook my head.

"This is so weird, but right on the first day that I had seen you, I had felt a strange connection to you. It was something unexplainable. In a room full of random strangers, I had noticed you. It was not like I immediately became enamored by you, but a thought had come into my head that someday you will play an important part in my life, and that I had to do what I could to stay in touch with you."

Sandxira continued to look at me.

"I probably would not have given it much thought, if my friend Xeala had not asked me about you, and kind of set in motion the chain of events. I confess that what had started out as a trivial thing, grew in my mind into something deeper and more meaningful.

"I have never believed that my fate was governed by forces beyond my control, but when you asked me to meet you when I was back in the city, I felt like I was the luckiest person on the planet, to get the chance to be able to spend some time with you. And after everything that we have been through together, now that we are at this crossroads and you have made your decision, as much as I might pretend to be okay with it, I am not and I really really wish that things could be different. And I once again feel the influence of those forces on my destiny, uncontrollable forces that has left me powerless and unable to do anything about our situation."

"I understand, but my purpose is greater than you or me." Sandxira said.

"I know. This almost makes me wish that choice based multiverses were a possibility, and there is some version of my universe, that is out there, where you have decided differently. I wish that there was some version of you out there who had decided to remain mortal."

"I am sorry for this."

I looked at Sandxira with a pained expression on my face. I put on a difficult smile, feeling like the soldier from 'One', who had heard a joke, just before the doctors pulled the plug on him.

We sat there facing each other. Outside, the sun rose to the zenith of its orbit, and momentarily stood there, before resuming its long lazy journey towards dusk.

~

I reached home, undressed, took out my phone and called Xeala.

I had never really liked the caller tune Xeala had installed on her phone. It was a cheerful, annoying and uninspiring travel song that was the opposite of my brooding heavy metal preferences, and was in conflict with my dark mood.

"What's up?" she asked.

"Sorry that I could not call you back yesterday." I apologized.

"How did it go with Sandxira?" She asked.

"Not great, to be honest. You were quite perceptive about what Sandxira wanted to talk about."

"Oh honey, I am so sorry."

"Its fine, I am okay with it. It was difficult, but I have managed to come to terms with it."

"I wish I could be there for you."

"It is okay. I am just glad that you are here with me on the call now."

"I know this is easy for me to say this as an outsider, and it may seem callous to you at the moment, but with time this will heal. You will forget about Sandxira, and something different, maybe something better will come into your life." Xeala said.

We paused speaking on the phone for a few seconds.

"It is kind of frustrating." I said.

"What is?" Xeala asked.

"That with time you get over a person and you forget what that person meant to you. I know deep down that is what is going to happen with Sandxira on a long enough timeline, and that is what should happen. But the truth is, I don't want that. Somehow this turmoil makes me feel alive. Without it, I am like a husk of a person, going through the motions. That is what is frustrating." I said.

"I never pegged you as an idealist." Xeala said.

"I don't know what I am anymore," I said, "you remember that time I told you about this girl back in college that I liked for five years? I thought that the feeling was real, not a passing infatuation. But there did come a time when the feeling was gone. It was a few months before she and I had that fight about her boyfriend, but neverthe-less that feeling was gone then and is gone now. And there are times when I wonder why I felt that way about her, but I never have an answer for myself, except that once upon a time, I just did. I have no memory of those feelings for that girl, except for the quantifiable recollection that such feelings persisted for a period of five years. I don't want the same thing to happen with Sandxira. I don't want to forget that feeling, but I know that given enough time, I will."

There was another brief pause.

"Did Sandxira say why?" Xeala asked.

"She did, yes. Unfortunately, I cannot tell you why. I am really sorry that I am coming across as this secretive asshole, but I want to respect her decision and do not want anyone to form any unflattering opinion of her."

"I understand."

"Thanks, Xeala. I hope you are okay with me not telling you."

"I am, absolutely. Far be it for me to get in the middle of what you two have decided."

"Thank you for your compassion and understanding. You still are my number one girl. And I am sorry that I have not been a nicer friend to you."

"You have been plenty nice. Who was it that I dragged off to have drinks with me at 12 a.m. in the night, even though he had gotten out of a tiring day at work and had to go back in early the next day?"

"It was I."

"Who was it, that stayed awake with me with me through the night, when I was deathly sick and took care of me, and then got me admitted to the hospital?"

"It was I."

"Who was my willing partner in all the crazy ideas that I came up with?"

"It was I."

"Damn right you it was you. You are an incredible person and have been an awesome friend. Nothing you say or do can take that feeling I have for you, away." Xeala said.

"Thanks, Xeala."

"I love you, babe."

"I love you too."

~

I was standing on the stairwell outside my office, looking out at the city skyline outside. The building I was in, was among the tallest in the surrounding area. The city has a distinct lack of buildings that were more than six storeys high as far as the eye could see. It would be incredibly inconvenient and challenging for a web slinging superhero to fight crime in this city.

I felt a tap on my shoulder and turned around to see Natascha standing next to me.

"What is up with you, boss?" she asked, "you seem more distracted than usual."

"Just a few things on my mind." I replied.

"Did you eat your lunch today?" Natascha asked.

I looked at her and smiled. I had never noticed how bright her eyes were. She proceeded to lean on the staircase next to me.

"Big Brother giving you trouble again?" I asked her. Big Brother was Natascha and my affectionate nickname for the head of the firm that she and I worked in.

"Not really, he has eased off for now. I have a new agreement to work on, so taking a breather before I go in."

"I see."

"I got into a big fight with my boyfriend last night." Natascha said.

Natascha had never been very reserved about sharing details of her personal life with people that she felt she was close to. There were times when you ran out of combinations of words to empathize with her. Only so many times could you say, "damn", "he doesn't deserve you" or the classic and dependable, "that bastard" and get away with it.

"What did he do this time?" I asked.

Maybe a slight tone of exasperation had inadvertently crept into my voice, for Natascha looked mildly affronted. However, she did not let that stop her.

"I confessed to him that I had a mild crush on this other guy that I met on a trekking trip last month, which I went on with some friends. He got upset over it, and we got into a huge fight that ended with him telling me to do whatever the hell I wanted to do." She said.

"Oh..."

"I feel bad though. My boyfriend is a really sweet guy, and he lets me be who I want to be, but there are times when he can be unreasonable and possessive."

"Sounds like a douche."

"He really is not. Even I know that it probably was not proper of me to feel any attraction towards that guy at the trek, but sometimes, in such surroundings, you cannot help yourself. Not that anything happened between us."

"I believe you."

"I wanted to come clean to him, because the guilt was eating at me. I was hoping that he would understand and not react the way he did." Natascha said.

"Maybe your boyfriend was feeling powerless being away from you in a different city. Even the strongest relationships suffer difficulties when distance comes in between."

"It has been a few months since he last visited." Natascha said.

"And not to play the devil's advocate here, but sometimes, it is okay to act on your instincts, and to tell the person you are seeing, that you do not have the same feelings for him anymore."

"Play the what?"

"Devil's advocate. It means someone who tries to side with both parties in an argument, just to make them consider and discuss it in more detail."

"I know what a devil's advocate is, don't mansplain to me. I could not hear what you had said the first time, that is why I asked you to repeat it."

"Oh... I am sorry for that." I apologized.

"It is okay." Natascha forgave me.

"However, regardless of everything, it is important to cherish what you do have instead of chasing after something that you may potentially do." I said.

"What happened to you? Why are you talking like a mentor figure in a daytime soap opera?" Natascha was curious.

"This girl I had been seeing, Sandxira, broke up with me."

"Oh... I am sorry."

"Its fine."

"What happened between you guys?" Natascha asked.

"She had some things to take care of, some plans that could not involve me. So..." I shrugged.

"What could such plans possibly be?"

"She had to travel back to her home dimension and take up work exploring other universes."

"Yeah right." Natascha said sarcastically.

I shrugged again.

"Its fine. I have made peace with it. There is nothing that could have been done."

Natascha patted me on the shoulder.

"Thanks." I said.

"Care to come out for a drink tonight?" she asked.

"I would love to." I said.

~

In a few hours' time Natascha and I got out of the office building and began walking towards a pub that was a few blocks away. I was apprehensive whether we would be getting a table, but Natascha assured me that this place that she was taking me to, was still under the radar of the pub hopping people, and it would be relatively easy to get in.

The place was called Tardy's. It seemed that the proprietor was a big fan of dated science fiction television shows and liked his puns. As imaginative as the title was, the decor was the opposite and was one that could be found dime a dozen in pubs throughout the country. The floor was wood paneled, the walls were painted a dark green color that was not favored by the dim lighting inside, and the chairs had been carved out of whisky barrels. The walls were adorned with movie posters through the ages, most of them lurid horror movies with low production values and gaudy props, reminiscent of the Hammer Horror films. Some knick knacks that friends and family members of the pub owner had picked up on their travels, had been used to spice up the place and elevate the decor of the drinking establishment.

We found a booth to ourselves. Looming down upon us was the poster of a cape wearing skeleton sitting at a piano, its hand raised in the air as if it was about to pounce on the piano keys with righteous vengeance. Next to the skeleton, a captive maiden was staring at us, her hands on her cheeks, ample bosom peeking out of her low-cut gown, her mouth transfixed in a silent scream, and her eyes bulging out. It would have been a more appropriate creative choice to provide the skeleton with a pipe organ instead of a piano, to elevate the sense of doom and gloom. Such movies were perfect viewing accompaniment for a night like this, when you were out drinking with friends.

Natascha picked up the laminated beverage menu, flipped it over a couple of times, and asked me, "What will you drink?"

"I usually prefer beer" I said, "but I am in the mood for something stronger today."

The pub did appear to be under the radar of people. Natascha and I were two of the few patrons, in an otherwise empty place, but the establishment did appear to have a steady footfall nevertheless. One of the plastic corners of the menu had already become dog eared, the lamination layers having been separated from each other.

I took the menu from Natascha and studied it, hoping to come across any cleverly named beverages that the owner had come up with, as a continued display of the skills that he had put into use while naming the pub. I was sadly disappointed to find that the owner's imagination was limited only to coming up with the name Tardy's, and the beverages on the menu had woefully generic names.

I order a double peg of whisky for myself, and Natascha ordered vodka. She liked to think of herself as being related in spirit to our friends from the freezing north.

"Thanks for this," I said, "I really could use a drink."

"You looked like you needed it, and it has been some time since I have come out for a drink as well." Natascha said.

"I thought your friends and you had sleepover drinking parties, didn't you?" I said.

"We used to, but it has been some time since the last one. Two of my friends are preparing for the upcoming judicial services examinations, and another has recently moved away to a different city for her job. It is just not the same without all five of us together."

"You could still have a drink sometime with the fifth one standing."

"Between you and me, she is a bit of a prude, and rarely drinks at all, other than a peg or so during our sleepover parties. She is not the most ideal drinking buddy."

"Glad I made the cut then." I said.

Our drinks had arrived. The fancy nature of the establishment became clear, when the waiter brought over one peg of my whisky in a glass, with the second peg in a smaller shot glass, in case I did not want to have both pegs at the same time. Unfortunately, Natascha's vodka had not received any such distinguished treatment. A tub filled with ice cubes was also placed on our table along with the beverages.

"Cheers," I said, and Cheers she said. We both clinked our glasses.

I had forgotten how strong whisky could be, and the first sip burned its way through my esophagus. Luckily enough, I was able to stifle back a cough, which would have caused the whisky to go down the wrong pipe and bring the evening to an abrupt end.

"This is nice," Natascha said, "you and I have never come out for a drink."

"That is true" I said

"In fact, you and I have barely hung out, outside of office hours."

"I am really glad that you are in this office though. It gets really weird around here sometimes. People are so needlessly serious, like cracking one joke would draw strict censure from everyone."

"I know what you mean. On my first day here, I tried to engage in idle chitchat with a couple of colleagues, who seemed approachable folks, but their seeming enthusiasm quickly devolved into curt replies to my enthusiastic jibber jabber. I was quite discouraged to approach anyone after that day." she said.

"Yes. One of the super seniors had asked me conversationally if I was fitting in, and whether I was able to engage in banter with anyone. I had to uncertainly reply to her saying, 'Is there someone like that in this office?'" I made an incredulous expression with my face.

Natascha laughed.

"Thanks for not giving up on me though," I continued, "I am really glad to have met you here."

"As am I," she said, "I feel that people here only talk to you when they expect to get something out of you, and are not inclined or interested in being your friend just for the sake of it."

I took a sip of my whisky and put it down.

"You know," I said, "My father had told me before I went off to college, to always remain friends with those from school and cherish them, because every friend you make after you pass out of school, would be out of some selfish personal interest. I am so glad that his hypothesis has been disproved, especially in this office."

"Yes. But one thing is odd though. Whenever you are not in office, people always come to me and enquire about your whereabouts, as if they expect me to always be aware of your movements." said Natascha.

"I know what you mean," I concurred, "the other day I overheard one of our paralegal personnel asking another whether Natascha would be coming to office. I think you had taken the day off. The latter promptly referred the former to me and asked him to check with me for any information about you."

"It's almost like they think that something is going on between us."

"I think that is because you *are* kind of like my work wife."

"A what now?"

"A work wife. Am I allowed to mansplain?" I asked.

"I will allow it in this instance." said Natascha with a mockingly haughty expression on her face.

"Thanks. A work wife or a work spouse is someone you are platonically close to at your work place. It is someone with whom you occasionally flirt, and who flirts back with you, without anything serious going on between the two of you. It is totally innocent and harmless."

"That is just ridiculous," Natascha said and laughed.

"It is quite a common concept. You and I confide in each other about professional matters. I am the first person you seek out when something goes wrong at work or you get to know of a juicy gossip, and you always tell me things about your personal relationship."

"I had never looked at it that way." Natascha confessed.

I nodded sagely, "When something or someone is bothering me at work, you are always there to listen to my rants, you come to me for guidance when you need help with something, and we can be silly with each other, and make uninhibited ribald jokes." I said.

"You are right, we indeed do all of the above."

At this point, I realized that Natascha had finished her drink and was stirring an empty glass with her stirrer, waiting for me to finish. I saw the dregs of whisky that was still in my glass, and downed them in a quick gulp. My esophagus had gotten accustomed to the burn by then. I waved to the waiter and asked him to repeat our drinks.

"I am sorry that I was not able to be as forthcoming about my relationship troubles with you, as you were with me." I said to Natascha.

"Its fine. I understand that you may not feel as comfortable sharing things with me as I feel in sharing things with you."

"It's just that the circumstances are so odd and, to an extent, outlandish, I doubt myself whether I have been able to come to terms with it or fully understand it."

"How come?"

"Let's just say that it is very humbling to know how insignificant you might be in the scheme of all of existence, and that, to reiterate a cliche, the needs of the many outweigh the needs of the few or the one."

"You are getting oddly cryptic and existential these hoss, how many drinks have you had?" Natascha grinned.

I lightly punched her on her shoulder.

"There were some things that Sandxira and I could not see eye to eye on. She wanted some things and I wanted completely different things. Being with me prevented Sandxira from being able to do what needed to be done."

"Like seeing other people?"

"No no," I laughed lightly, "I am talking about some work commitments that she had, which would require her to travel."

"Could you guys not have made long distance work?"

"Probably not, too many variables have become involved, and being with me would acutely prevent her from fulfilling her commitments. She had said, that given a choice, without any encumbrances, she would have chosen me over them, but I too realized that such commitments of hers are incredibly important, and I cannot stand in her way." I was holding my glass during this time, turning it around and observing it keenly as the etchings on the glass reflected the light.

"I understand." said Natascha.

"I am sorry if this sounds cliched and banal."

"Its fine. Cliches are handy, they do the job. The reason that cliches become cliches is that they are the hammers and screwdrivers in the toolbox of communication"

I turned and looked at Natascha. She shrugged.

"I read it in a book once." she said.

"Touché" I said.

The waiter had brought back our drinks refilled, and had blended back into his designated corner of the pub, till he was to be summoned again.

"I am glad we are out today," I said, "you have been really supportive."

"It's the least I could do for my work husband." Natascha said and winked.

"I am really lucky to have met you here. You have made me look forward to come to office even on days when I absolutely do not want to. Thanks for being there."

"You are most welcome, dear," she said, patting my shoulder, "and the next time you say anything like this, I am taking away your whisky".

"Fair enough" I said and laughed.

The skeleton in the poster above our table was starting to look a lot less intimidating now. We ordered one more round of drinks after that, and spent the rest of the evening dissing our co-workers and judging them for their various eccentricities. There were a few more close calls for me in the burning alcohol going down the wrong pipe department. I had forgotten how funny Natascha could be at times, when she lets loose.

We were just adequately inebriated, hitting the sweet spot between being tempted to make fools of ourselves on the one hand, and chilling and listening to blues rock music that made us feel like we had seen God, on the other. To the pub's credit, the owners had cracked that code, and saxophone versions of classic rock songs were starting to play on the speakers.

We paid our bill and got out of Tardy's. Natascha had booked a taxi through an app and we stood on the sidewalk waiting for the taxi driver to lose his way, end up heading into a blind lane, not ask for directions due to misplaced pride and arrogance, rely on the faulty onboard navigation, and finally reach someplace a kilometer away from the pick-up spot, from where he would call Natascha saying that he had arrived at the designated location.

"Have you booked a taxi for yourself?" Natascha asked.

"I feel like walking a little. Maybe I will walk to the bus terminus and take some transport from there." I said.

"Okay."

A light breeze had begun to blow in from a large lake that was a few hundred meters away from Tardy's. The lake was the crown jewel of the office locality, a wide expanse of serene water nestled among the concrete towers of the workforce.

"I have never been to that lake," I said pointing at the body of water.

"Neither have I. We rarely get out of office at an early hour, so that we are able to take time and roam about, and when we do get out of office early, we are in too much of a rush to reach home or make good on other plans with friends." Natascha said philosophically, "Maybe you can seduce one of the countless women who work in these office buildings, and bring her here on a date." she continued.

"I can probably do that, thanks for the encouragement, but I will need you to be my wing lady and facilitate it." I said.

"Done deal. I will need to verify and see whom I am handing off my work husband to." Natascha said.

By now Natascha's taxi driver had reached the designated one-kilometer-away-from-the-actual-pick-up-spot location and had started calling her. She was able to guide the taxi to where we were standing.

"See you tomorrow." she said brightly. She gave me a side hug and got into her taxi.

"Message me when you reach" I said, as she waved while her taxi pulled out onto the road. Her wave turned into a thumbs up of acknowledgment.

I stood there for a few seconds, then took out my earphones, plugged them in, and hit play on my phone to a seminal punk rock song about walking lonely roads. Then, silhouetted in the moonlight, I began walking towards the bus terminus.

PART 12: CLANGING OF WHEELS

Sandxira and I were sitting in a tram, travelling through one of the main roads in the city. The tram network was one of the oldest ones that was still operational, in the country. It had started out with more than twenty five tram lines that were spread throughout the city, but since the advent of faster modes of transportation, the trams had found themselves gradually becoming outdated. They were no more the main lifeline of the city and were relegated to cater to pleasure trips for tourists who sought to soak in the heritage of the city, while travelling at a leisurely pace. There were only six operational tram lines in the city at present. The trams held onto their waning legacy by permitting themselves to be romanticized in motion pictures that were shot in the city.

The tram that we were sitting in, was a double coach one, having a driver up front in the first coach, and the second coach was connected to the first by a vestibule. The tram car was powered by direct current power supply from electric lines that ran overhead. The tram had a very unique rhythm to it as it moved over the tracks, and every time the gear shifted and the tram changed speed, the internal machinery of the tram heavily thudded and clanked, like the opening credits of Hellboy II: The Golden Army.

Fortunately, the tram line that we were travelling on, ran through the main road which was connected to the arterial lane where Sandxira's apartment was. It was the last week that Sandxira was going to be here, in this city, in this dimension, in this universe. We were trying to spend the last few days apart in order to make the eventual departure easier for both of us. Sandxira had mentioned to me, when we first met nearly three years ago, that she wanted to travel in a tram around the city. I wanted this tram ride to be my departure gift to her.

She was wearing a blue dress that day, which looked like it was made of denim. The dress was tied around her waist with a blue belt of the same material. I had decided to go in for a grey shirt with black denim trousers for the day.

The tram was never crowded at any time of the day, and when we got in, it was easy to find seats, which were lined against the coach wall, so that you sat with your back to the tram window and had to turn around in your seat to be able to look outside.

"Thanks for seeing me today." I said.

"It was the least I could do." Sandxira said.

I smiled. "There is no way we can stay in touch, right?" I asked.

She shook her head.

"You are sure of this." I said, more as a statement than a question.

She nodded.

The tram conductor was intermittently blowing his whistle, as the tram came to a halt at some places to pick up passengers.

"Where do you want to go? What plans do we have for the day?" Sandxira asked.

"This tram route circumvents nearly the entire city." I said, "I was hoping that we could travel all the way in this tram till the terminus and then come back the same way. Just like you had told me that you wanted to do, way back when we first met."

She laughed. It was the same throaty lilting laugh that had enamored me. "Are you serious?" She asked.

"Yes."

"You want to go to the terminus and come back?"

"Yes."

"That's it?"

"Yes."

"Okay, I guess we will do that for the day then. But why though?" Sandxira asked.

"I don't know. I just wanted to spend the day with you in one place, without going through the trouble of running around, going to a restaurant, sitting through a movie or doing any strenuous activity." saying this, I winked.

Sandxira smiled. "What about food?" she asked.

"We'll get food from whichever vendor comes aboard with his fares."

"Do you have enough money for tickets?"

"I think we are good. Time stopped for the tram network nearly fifty years ago, and so did the hike in fares."

"Fair enough. For a moment I thought you were going to say that you robbed a bank or something."

"That was my initial thought, but then I remembered that I am not a hack."

Sandxira laughed again. We sat on the tram and began to travel through the city. We were frequently overtaken by cars and buses that had the benefit of running on faster engines. Even though the day was sunny, the temperature in the city had fallen due to rain showers the week before. The fans in the tram were adequate to keep the heat at bay. I was turned halfway in my seat and facing Sandxira, and she was turned halfway in her seat facing me. In the vacant seat between us, a pile of empty packets was slowly growing. The martyrs included peanuts, roasted chickpeas, salted fruits, snack mix and even a packet of lozenges. Fortunately, Sandxira had picked up the excellent practice of travelling with a bottle of water, which helped immensely in preemptively alleviating the inevitable heartburn that would have followed the consumption of such spicy foods. However, I still failed to suppress an audible burp that turned some heads among the other passengers.

"Sorry," I said covering my mouth with my hand, looking embarrassed.

"Are you okay?" Sandxira asked.

"Yeah yeah. It was merely a small disruption." I assured her, "My family has allegedly descended from a holy ascetic who was infamous in the scriptures for his gluttony. Legend has it that he drank an entire ocean till the last drop.'"

She raised an eyebrow.

"It is a joke. I like to crack it from time to time. I have no way of tracing my ancestors all the way to the scriptures."

"Do you never feel curious to find out?"

"Not really. A wise man had said to me once that you should not ask questions you do not want to know the answers to."

"Let me guess, this was from a movie?" said **Sandxira**, sardonically.

I tapped my nose to indicate that she was correct.

"That and another movie where the well-meaning actions of the protagonist leads to his girlfriend finding out that one of her ancestors was a notorious serial killer, has put me off any such curiosity to go digging after my past. Ironically the latter movie was a romantic comedy." I said.

Sandxira nodded.

"What about you?" I asked, "What is your story?"

"Let's see..." she said, and proceeded to tell me the history of her people. To be honest, it was too controversial and incomprehensible for our human minds with our set rules and morals to grasp, and I am not sure I understand a lot of it myself. If we were in a movie or any other form of visual media, this would be the part where the voices of the characters would fade out, the background music would soar, and the censorious dialogues would be communicated by the characters to each other through exaggerated hand gestures. I began regretting my supercilious advice to myself from a few minutes ago, when I said that one should not ask questions one does not want to know the answers to. There could be a slight chance that Sandxira was making these up in an effort to throw me off, so that it would be easier for us to depart. After a while, my high tolerance for absurdity kicked in and her tales became palatable. You tend to develop such a tolerance when you read outlandish graphic novels written by auteurs, who claim that the world is secretly run by inter-dimensional giant scorpion gods. Which reminded me...

"Tell me something. In all your travels, have you or any of your, for lack of a better term, brethren, come across any race of scorpion gods in any universe, that are hell-bent on dominating the multiverse?" I asked.

"Where did you get that from?" Sandxira asked.

"Just curious, came into my mind all of a sudden."

"Not that we know of, yet."

"What about a universe where a creator brought the holy ones into existence with his thought, and who in turn played music to please him and, in the process, wove the universe into existence with their melody?"

"Is this what we are doing now?" Sandxira asked me with an upward curl of her left lip.

"While I still have you here with me, I was wondering if I could pick your mind to see if any of the fictional universes that I have read about, seen or heard of, have any basis in reality." I shrugged.

"What would that achieve?"

"A deeper respect on my part for the creators of such works, who so accurately predicted such seemingly fictional universes, despite possibly having no access to the multiverse."

"Are you not afraid of being disappointed?" she asked.

"I will learn to live with it." I said.

Sandxira seemed to be considering in her mind to what extent she could give out such information about the multiverse, and whether it would break my sanity.

"Okay, shoot," she said, after some time, "and in response to your previous question, yes, there is such a universe that has been woven from music".

If there was an Ainuric choir behind me, this was the moment that they would have start singing in a heavenly chorus. Maybe I could hire one, once humans discovered the secrets of inter-dimensional travel.

"What about a universe where the galaxy is run by a feudal empire and everyone trades in spice, which has become the most valuable commodity?"

"Nope." she said.

"What about a universe which is overrun by moon sized monsters that are hell bent on consuming all sentient life?"

"Imaginative, but no. We have not met any beings yet, that are hellbent on anything, least of all leather." and saying so Sandxira winked.

"Ahh... I see you have been brushing up on your Judas Priest." I said with a smile.

She made a gesture of doffing an imaginary hat.

"What about a realm of black stars and non-euclidian celestial bodies that is ruled by an entity wearing a yellow garb?" I asked.

Sandxira shook her head.

"What about a steampunk universe inhabited by creatures such as humanoid cacti, mosquito human hybrids with paddle like wings, sentient hedgehogs, humans with scarab heads, vampires, gargoyles and centaurs?"

"There are numerous steampunk universes, but none specifically with the combination of creatures co-existing together as you mentioned."

"I was really counting on that one." I said, a little disheartened, "What about..."

And so, the grilling of Sandxira continued. The sun was progressively making its way across the sky. We had fortunately taken a side which was spared from the sun's ire, as the tram made its way through the city, towards its end point. After a couple of hours, we soon found ourselves entering a tram yard, having reached the last destination of the tram route. The vehicle had emptied itself by the time the terminus arrived, and we were the only two people sitting inside.

The conductor made his way towards us. "Last stand." he said.

"It is okay, we will be going back the same way." I said.

He shrugged and said, "This tram will leave from here in fifteen minutes". Then he proceeded to nonchalantly get down from the running tram and headed to the office to submit the earnings from the route. It was a good thing that people in this city were not intrusive or judgmental.

We stepped out of the tram and stretched, having been sitting inside for a long time.

"This was a lot of fun." Sandxira admitted, "Thanks for planning this."

"I am glad you enjoyed it," I said, "but to be honest, I was hoping to bargain with you."

"What about?"

"I know that I have no right to ask this of you, but I was really hoping that this tram ride would not be my farewell gift to you."

"What do you mean?"

"Why don't I tell you on our way back?" I asked. Sandxira assented.

We crossed the road to a shop on the opposite side of the street, outside the tram depot and stocked up on supplies for our return trip. I was quite excited to find that the shopkeeper sold gold chocolate coins. They used to be a delicacy when I was a kid. The quality of the chocolate inside was not always great, but we were all drawn to the gold cover that the chocolates came wrapped in, like Smaug the dragon, attracted to a mound of treasure, or pirates lusting after gold doubloons. It was a nice piece of nostalgia. Sadly though, there were no versions of the multiverse that Sandxira's people had come across, in which dragons existed.

The tram conductor from before had spotted us across the street, for he shouted to catch our attention and let us know that the tram was leaving. We hurried back with our arms full of supplies, and climbed on. We headed back to our previous seats, but exchanged them so that we could continue to have the view of each other in the same backdrop from as before.

"So, what was it that you wanted to bargain with me about?" Sandxira enquired.

"You know, I had stayed back in our work city for a few days, after moving out of the last job. I had this notion in my head that before I leave, I wanted to view the perfect sunset, one where the setting sun would continue towards the horizon uninterrupted and unhindered, to where the sky and sea meet, till its bottom would touch the surface of the sea, and it would gently ease itself into its twilight bath. The sun would eventually give out a brief flicker of greenish light before being submerged into the depths of the sea, waiting to rise anew to a new day."

"Wow... that is beautiful."

"Thank you," I said, "I am glad to say, that due to the benevolence of some cosmic consciousness that I have begun to I believe in, my efforts succeeded a few days before I was supposed to leave the city, when I found myself on Dahanu beach near a fishing village. On that beach I was treated to the most amazing sunset of all time, which occurred exactly the way as I described it."

Her hand brushed against mine, and I noticed that she had goosebumps.

"At that moment, as I sat there looking at the star, for some reason your face came into my mind. Maybe it was an odd premonition, but I realized, there was no one else that I wanted to share that moment with more, than with you. I wanted you to be by my side, as together, we would watch the most perfect sunset."

She reached out and held my hand.

"I was wondering, if, before you go, we could try doing that sometime."

Sandxira was silent for a while.

"I am not sure if that would be a good idea." she said finally.

I let out a sigh, turned away from her, my back to the tram window and spread out my legs in front of me.

"Fair enough," I said and I sat looking at my feet, pensively.

She leaned forward and put her arm around my neck. I reached up and touched her arm with my hands. No matter how aloof people in this city pretended to be, such public displays of affection were always met with a few judgmental stares, especially from the middled aged women, if they happened to be nearby.

Evening had started to fall, as the tram made its way across the grounds that were close to Sandxira's office. The sky had turned a cobalt blue shade, as street lights lining the side of the tram tracks began to light up. Following suit, the inside of the tram also lit up with a golden yellow light from tungsten bulbs. The sound of cars and buses passing us, carrying passengers back to their homes after the long day at work, began to get louder, as the tram entered the main thoroughfare enroute to its other depot. Quite soon, we arrived at the stop close to Sandxira's apartment.

"Thanks for today," she kissed me on the cheek, and stood up, "I am going to miss you."

"As will I." I said.

She gingerly stepped off the tram and onto the road. The tram was stuck at a traffic signal, along with the rest of the vehicles on the road.

She stood by the side of the road, looking at me and I sat in the tram looking back at her. The rest of the passengers were waiting for signal to open and for the tram to leave, but I was secretly wishing for a malfunction in the traffic light kiosk.

Just as the signal was about to open, Sandxira suddenly stepped forward, climbed back onto the tram and came and sat down beside me.

"Woah! Was that not your stop?" I asked.

"I can always get down at the next stop and walk back." She said.

"Okay, I guess."

The tram trudged to life, as the traffic signal became green, and began to lazily move along the track.

"Four days later is supposed to be my last day here. Why don't we take a trip to the beach that day, see if we can treat ourselves to a sunset, and maybe then I can leave?" Sandxira said.

"Okay!" I said in a tone that was a tad more excited than I meant it to.

"Great! See you then." she said, and then got down in a trot from the slowly moving tram.

I put my head out of the window and looked back at her, as she waved, before the tram turned a corner, and she became hidden from view.

PART 13: BYE BYE BYE REPRISE/ OOGWAY ASCENDS

On the designated day, I found myself outside Sandxira's apartment. I rang the bell and she opened the door smiling. She smelt like lavender that day.

As I stepped in, I saw that the entire apartment was barren. All the fixtures had been removed. The dining table and chairs were gone. The refrigerator had been disconnected and probably sold, leaving a bright patch behind, that stood out when compared to the rest of the wall, which had been darkened by the soot and oil from the kitchen. Sandxira's bedroom was empty too. The square footage of the room was impressive, I realized at that moment and the adjective "gargantuan" did not do it justice. An empty can of lavender perfume rolled around in a corner of her bedroom. Sandxira had decided to not let any of her mortal possessions go to waste. Only the drapes on the windows were still left. They seemed to be reluctantly moving in the breeze, as if mourning the absence of a companion who had been with them for a long time.

"Just in time. I am done here. Shall we leave?" she asked.

I took one last look around the place where Sandxira and I had spent so many nights together. "Let's go." I said.

I was not surprised to see that Sandxira was not carrying any luggage with her. You cannot really carry any with you in your inter-dimensional travels.

The beach was around two hours away from the city, and regular buses plied on the route every half an hour. A small community of people from different social strata lived near the coast. They came to the city in the morning for their jobs. Some worked in various posts in offices, some were household maids and some came with the fish and seafood they had caught from the sea, to sell in the market places. The workforce had completed their jobs and their sales for the day, and were headed back home in the buses. There were others too who, like us, were travelling to the beach to spend the evening there. The fishermen were precariously perched on the roof of the bus, owing to the reluctance of the general public to put up with the stench of fish. Everyone else had orderly queued up for the buses, and rushed in to occupy seats every time a bus came to a stop in front of them. Half an hour later, we got out of the city and onto the highway that would take us to the beach. The traffic was quite heavy, and the bus came to frequent halts despite travelling on the highway. It was only in the last fifteen kilometers leg of the journey that it became smooth sailing, and the bus traveled at speeds that its engineers, in all their infinite wisdom, had designed it to.

"This was a good decision." Sandxira said. Her head was half an inch out of the window, her hair flying in the wind. I was beginning to taste the slightly salty air of the sea.

"I am glad you wanted to do this." I said. **Sandxira** pulled her head in, looked at me and smiled.

"Can I ask you something?" I queried.

"Some other question about the multiverse?" her eyes twinkled mischievously.

"Not really. It is about humanity. You have lived among us for so long. I guess it is safe to assume that you have formed your own opinions about us."

"Go on." she said.

"It is kind of a question that I have asked you already. I know that you cannot provide answers to our future, but you have seen our civilization progress. Do you feel that someday we can reach the stars or become inter-dimensional explorers ourselves? I am asking you to tell me based on the conclusions that you have drawn, purely from your personal perspective."

Sandxira pondered over the question for a while. Then she said, "To be fair, it does seem like you guys are in a bit of rut right now."

"What do you mean?" I asked.

"Well, there have not been a lot of major scientific breakthroughs have there? Not a lot of money is spent on research and development, but an awful lot is being spent on defence, as if all the countries expect to go to war with each other at the drop of a hat. The biggest innovation in the past fifteen years has been the advent of social media. That is probably the most game changing and disruptive event. What was once cool and niche, has become mainstream and dominant now. Granted that there are some benefits to technology as social media has provided voices to the unheard, made it easier let your opinion be known and has, in turn, been used to hold people accountable, but on the flip side, social media can also be used to spread hatred, meddle in democracies and bully people. Then there is the whole breach of privacy issue. I think these days its cons have begun to outweigh its pros."

"You have a fair point there." I said.

"Instead of your best minds being engaged in building flying cars, undertaking inter-stellar mining and or working on deep space exploration, they are engaged in trying to figure out how to put animal filters on human faces, while they wait for their shares to vest. You cannot really blame them too. That is where the money is and at the end of the day that is what matters. It is only a tiny handful of people who seek to innovate and build something new. Most others are simply following tried and tested formulas to build wealth for themselves. I also feel that culturally humanity is becoming bank-rupt, with people using powerful resources for sowing discord, creating divides and pushing their own selfish agendas, instead of thinking of humanity as a gestalt, as a unified race with a common goal. Hopefully this bankruptcy is temporary."

"How do we get out of this rut? Become culturally relevant again?"

Sandxira shrugged, "I feel that humanity should be willing to take more risks," she said, "have a daring vision to achieve something outlandish, and above all, have a strong sense of what is ethical and moral. It is good to be competitive, but at what point do you give up your values in order to chase after money. It is a construct after all. Money should be a framework to live by, not the purpose of life itself. It's like you said in that song. You need to find the things that give you true happiness so that you do not become bitter and resentful in old age."

I began humming the guitar solo of Paranoid.

"Above all, humanity should reignite its sense of wonder; wonder at the cosmos, wonder in their capacity to do good and wonder at life itself. These are some things that might help." Sandxira said.

"So, there is hope for us to become interstellar travelers?" I asked.

"I think so. In the grand scheme of this universe and of humanity's existence itself, this despair that you see around you is but a small speck. If this planet's age is equivalent to what you understand as a calendar year, then humanity came into existence on December 31, and this rut is barely five minutes to ten o' clock." Sandxira said and smiled, "Maybe next time one of us is back in this realm, this entire planet will be surrounded by giant gateways, that act as wormholes to the deep reaches of space."

I was struck in the gut by the reminder of my impermanence, and the fact that it might be eons from now when anyone from Sandxira's universe will be back with us. However, her words gave me hope. I may not be around to see it, but humanity could one day still become a spacefaring race. It reminded me of Alfred Bester's poem:

"Gully Foyle is my name
And Terra is my nation.
Deep space my dwelling place,
The stars my destination."

As we reached closer to the beach, the bus slowed to a halt. The conductor shouted and let all the passengers know that the last stop was about to arrive. The regular travelers had already begun stepping out of the moving bus with a practiced ease. The bus wedged itself into the stand and came to a halt in a parking position.

The bus stand was on a slightly elevated cliff, as was the coastal settlement itself. A few meters away from the bus stand, a lane had gone down to the beach. The lane had quite a steep incline, and we saw tourists on their way back, huffing and puffing to the bus stand. Shops dotted the left side of the lane as we went downhill, while a brick wall acted as a boundary on the right side, separating the lane from a resort next door. Most of the shops sold various items designed to cater to tourists, such as straw hats, cheap sunglasses, paintings and photos of the beach, and some furniture made of palm trees. There were a few shops in between that sold water, crisps, biscuits and soft drinks for the thirsty and hungry visitors. The lane curved as it went down, so that it was only in the last few meters that we were able to get a glimpse of the beach.

The sands of the beach were black in color in some places due to the presence of ilmenite and monazite minerals. The beach was bordered on one side by the sea, and rows after rows of palm trees on the other side. On the southernmost and opposite side of the beach from where we had entered, there was a lighthouse, located on top of a hillock, providing visitors, who would dare to venture to the top with an even more expansive view of the surrounding areas. In the middle of the beach was a high rock promontory, that appeared to be the still standing ruins of an ancient building which had gone underwater when the sea moved closer to the coast. From a bird's eye view, the beach looked crescent shaped.

"Where do you want to sit?" I asked Sandxira.

"Let us sit on the sands somewhere?" she suggested.

We found a relatively clean stretch of sand that was not littered with food packets or empty bottles left behind by unconscientious tourists, and sat down. I sat with my legs folded under me in order to accommodate the stubborn paunch that refused to go yet, despite trying my hardest during workouts. Sandxira sat with her knees tucked in front of her.

The land breeze was blowing quite hard, and the hair on my head was standing on end, supported by the wind. The sky was starting to darken in the approaching evening, as the sun made its way towards the horizon, having completed its journey across the sky for the day.

I sighed, but this was not a sigh of sadness or reluctance. It was a sigh of acceptance.

"This is nice." I said.

"Yes, it is." Sandxira concurred.

We sat there looking at the sun as it slowly inched its way closer to the sea. Sandxira reached out with her hand towards me. After a moment's hesitation, I reached out and held it.

The lighthouse had been lit up in the gathering dusk, and was beginning to emit a rhythmic, eerie light from its rotating lamp.

It was a little disheartening when the sun was obstructed by a heretofore hidden patch of cloud as it nearly reached the sea, and began setting behind the cloud cover. There was a tiny bit of hope in me that the lower part of the setting sun would come out of the other side of the cloud cover at any moment, and still be able to keep its date with the sea. I was unfortunately disappointed, as the sun began gradually disappearing behind the cloud.

Sandxira squeezed my hand. I squeezed hers back. Then we let go of each other.

In the twilight, the lighthouse's rays had begun to cast an unearthly charm over the beach.

I sensed the sand moving next to me, as Sandxira stood up. I heard the gentle trudging of foot on sand, as I felt Sandxira walking away.

I closed my eyes, put my hands on my cheek and sat there motionless. The sound of sea gulls going back to their nests were echoing in the air. Garbled voices of tourists could be heard exclaiming how fantastic the place was. Despite all the noise around me, I felt like I had gone deaf. Sounds continued to come in, but none registered in my head.

The night got darker. I continued to sit where I was, as if in an ascetic trance, till I was jerked out of my daze by someone shaking me by the shoulder. I turned around to see a police officer in khakis looking at me. He was aggressively blowing his whistle but stopped when he saw my face. Despite being strangers, an unspoken understanding formed between us and he held me by the shoulder as he escorted me off the beach. It was closing time, he said, and no one was allowed to remain on the beach after 7 p.m. to avoid any untoward incidents.

"Come back tomorrow son. I hope you are able to come to peace with whatever is troubling you." the policeman said, and then waved at me. Still in my daze, I walked up to the bus stand and stood in queue to take the returning bus back to the city. The crowd had thinned and I was able to get a window seat to myself. The bus dropped me back to the place where it had picked us up, in front of Sandxira's home. Without acknowledging my surroundings, I got into a taxi and gave the driver the direction to my home.

I went into my bedroom and sat on the edge of my bed. My face was buried in my hands, my elbows resting on my legs. I saw blackness in front of me, interspersed with orange spots that formed over the darkness of my closed eyelids.

My phone suddenly buzzed. I waited for some time and took it out. I saw that it was a message from Natascha. It said, "Hey boss. Your work wife here. Just checking in on you. Hope everything is okay."

I looked at the message once again. I blinked a couple of times. Then I smiled.

"It is." I wrote back.

-FIN-

Author's Note:

Readers will notice that none of the cities mentioned in this book, have been named. This has been a deliberate decision, to allow me some creative liberty in designing the end of the story and modifying it to suit my prosaic needs. A lot of the readers will be able to guess the cities I am writing about, from the descriptions that are provided in the book; for instance, the trams, Palladian porches by the river side and the planetarium. For those who are curious to know the names of the actual cities, I have left small nuggets of reference to places within or near such cities, like "Dadar", "Manori", "Dahanu" and "Jadavpur". Looking up these places online will give you a fair idea of the places that I have based the story in.

I hope you, the reader, have enjoyed this small independent effort, brought to fruition with the help of a few friends. I thank you for allowing me to take you on a journey, through a story that is quite personal to me. I thank you for spending your hard-earned money in getting a copy of this book, when you had the option of spending it elsewhere, on possibly more important things. Last of all, I thank you for choosing this book and being invested in my story.

Acknowledgements

Author William Gibson, of the seminal cyberpunk masterpiece, "Neuromancer", has said in interviews that when he was commissioned to work on the book, and given a year's time to finish the manuscript, he wrote the entire thing in "blind animal panic". He did so in order to meet the deadline, having personally been under the impression that the work would take him at least four to five years to complete. A similar sentiment was in play in my mind when I started working on this book. Soon after the coronavirus outbreak took place in India and one of the harshest lockdowns in the world was implemented in the country, all of us began working from home, and ended up saving some additional time every day, that was normally taken up in commute. When April was ending and May was rolling in, it was announced on the news that the lockdown would be lifted in the beginning of June. While none of us had any idea how the Unlock(s) would eventually play out, there was a general impression that life would resume in a completely normal and pre-lockdown manner, which meant that we would be required to report to our offices and go back to spending an inordinate amount of time, travelling. It was with that realization, that I was seized with "blind animal panic". I had been planning to start work on a book for ages, but kept putting it off. I realized that it was now or never, and so I began working on my manuscript on May 1, 2020, and, much like Tom Cruise hitting a button at the end of a Mission Impossible movie and screaming, "Mission Accomplished", I finished the first draft of this book on June 1, 2020. While writing with a fire lit under your Greendale flag is not an ideal way to get work done, it does prove effective a lot of times, especially to motivate laid back people such as myself.

I wish to thank my Mother, Indrani Chakraborty, for creating me, for inadvertently cultivating in me a lifelong obsession with science fiction and for being incredibly patient and tolerant with me as I went through mood swings and acted out like an ungrateful prick while working on this book.

I wish to thank my Father, Ajoy Kumar Chakraborty, for cultivating the habit of reading in me and for enticing me with imaginative tales of the space adventures of Captain Ram and Vice-Captain Shyam (which I still believe were legitimate tales and not 'inspired' from Star Trek).

I wish to thank Shuchi Singh, for taking time out of her busy schedule, reading the manuscript and providing me with her invaluable inputs, which helped me mold this book from its fairly uneven earlier drafts into something that I feel pride in presenting to everyone. Without her encouragement and support, I would have never had taken up writing seriously, and for that I thank her.

I wish to thank Smriti Tripathi, for standing like a rock by my side through one of the most difficult times in my life, for introducing me to Nutella waffles, and for making me a better person. For all these things I thank her.

I wish to thank Abhinaya Chandran, who wanted to know the story that inspired this book, which made me put the tale down in writing to get some perspective on it and for that I thank her. I am also indebted to her for taking time out of her busy schedule, reading the manuscript and providing me with her invaluable inputs.

I wish to thank Saloni Sehgal for engaging her unique artistic sensibilities, implementing her vision and creating the incredible cover for this book. She made me realize that, sometimes a writer can be inflexibly fixated on his own vision, and a friend can bring to life a much better interpretation of his ideas, and for that I thank her.

Lastly, I wish to thank Sukriti Kashyap. Conversations with her, helped me realize that I was needlessly holding on to an ideal as well as selfish end to this story, whereas the rightful thing to do would be to let go. For that, I thank her.